den·im

(de-nim-)
noun

1. A DURABLE TWILLED
   CLOTH TYPICALLY IN BLUE

2. STAPLE IN EVERY GIRL'S WARDROBE

3. FASHION AND FUNCTION IN ONE
   BACKSIDE-FLATTERING FABRIC

4. THE DEADLIEST TEXTILE
   ON THE MARKET

no escape

Hand in hand we sprinted for the station, arriving out of breath just moments before the train was supposed to leave. The ticket windows were closed so we had to buy our tickets from the machines. It felt like forever that Mom was feeding coins into the slot and another eternity for the machine to print and spit out our tickets. We grabbed them and raced through the turnstile, reaching the train car just as the warning chimes sounded, signaling that the doors were about to close.

The train had already started to move by the time we settled into our seats. I leaned back against the upholstery, silently saying my good-byes to Lyon. Then I noticed Mom's grip on the armrest tighten and I followed her gaze out the window.

Marlboro Man was running onto the platform. Late. Too late. I smiled at his failure . . . until it hit me. My ticket. I flipped it over and my heart dropped. Ours was an express train. No stops between Lyon and Paris. He may have missed us, but he would know exactly where we were headed. And when we would get there.

One glance at Mom and I knew she was thinking the same thing.

We were in trouble.

LINDA GERBER'S *DEATH BY* SERIES

Death by Bikini

Death by Latte

Death by Denim

OTHER SLEUTH BOOKS YOU MAY ENJOY

DEATH BY DENIM

LINDA GERBER

SLEUTH
SPEAK
An Imprint of Penguin Group (USA) Inc.

For Nin

SLEUTH / SPEAK
Published by the Penguin Group
Penguin Group (USA) Inc., 345 Hudson Street, New York, New York 10014, U.S.A.
Penguin Group (Canada), 90 Eglinton Avenue East, Suite 700,
Toronto, Ontario, Canada M4P 2Y3 (a division of Pearson Penguin Canada Inc.)
Penguin Books Ltd, 80 Strand, London WC2R 0RL, England
Penguin Ireland, 25 St Stephen's Green, Dublin 2, Ireland (a division of Penguin Books Ltd)
Penguin Group (Australia), 250 Camberwell Road, Camberwell, Victoria 3124, Australia
(a division of Pearson Australia Group Pty Ltd)
Penguin Books India Pvt Ltd, 11 Community Centre,
Panchsheel Park, New Delhi - 110 017, India
Penguin Group (NZ), 67 Apollo Drive, Rosedale, North Shore 0632, New Zealand
(a division of Pearson New Zealand Ltd)
Penguin Books (South Africa) (Pty) Ltd, 24 Sturdee Avenue,
Rosebank, Johannesburg 2196, South Africa

Registered Offices: Penguin Books Ltd, 80 Strand, London WC2R 0RL, England

This Sleuth edition published by Speak,
an imprint of Penguin Group (USA) Inc., 2009.

3 5 7 9 10 8 6 4 2

LIBRARY OF CONGRESS CATALOGING-IN-PUBLICATION DATA
Gerber, Linda C.
Death by denim / Linda Gerber.—Sleuth ed.
p. cm.
Summary: Sixteen-year-old Aphra and her mother, a CIA agent, are hiding in France
after having been given new identities, but they must go on the run again
when their location is discovered by a dangerous criminal.
ISBN 978-0-14-241119-3 (pbk. : alk. paper) [1. Spies—Fiction. 2. Criminals—Fiction.
3. France—Fiction. 4. Italy—Fiction.] I. Title.
PZ7.G293567Def 2009
[Fic]—dc22
2008041322

Speak ISBN 978-0-14-241119-3

Printed in the United States of America

Acknowledgments

The writing of this book was made possible by the encouragement and support of my family who continue to be my number-one cheerleaders. Thanks, guys!

Also, special thanks to my CPs, Jen, Ginger, Barb, Nicole, Julie, Kate, Karen, and Marsha for their wisdom and patience, and to Davide and Natalie Lorenzi, Jonathan Neve, and Ammi-Joan Paquette for their generous language and translation help.

As always, I am indebted to the fantastic team at Puffin for bringing the book to life. Heartfelt thanks to Angelle Pilkington (welcome to the new addition!), Grace Lee (best of luck with nursing!), and Kristin Gilson (I appreciate the 11th hour save!) for their editorial genius, and to designers Theresa Evangelista and Linda McCarthy for their brilliant cover designs. It's been my sincere pleasure to work with the best people in the business!

DEATH BY DENIM

CHAPTER 1

I knew it was just a matter of time before they caught up with us. Knew it every morning as I kissed my mother good-bye and walked out the door. Knew it every afternoon as I rode my bike home from the school in Lyon, France, where I had enrolled under a counterfeit name. Knew it every minute of every day, so it shouldn't have hit me with such a jolt when I noticed the man following me. But it did.

Part of the shock, I suppose, was the realization that I'd seen him before. Despite all the rules and techniques my mom had tried to drill into my head since we'd slipped underground, his presence hadn't more than grazed my consciousness before. Looking back, I recognized how often he'd been in shadows or hovering around the periphery of my attention. It wasn't until he grew bold and walked right past me, though, that all the other sightings registered in my head. Then everything fell into place—*thunk, thunk, thunk, thunk*—like bars in a cage locking tight.

We'd been out to dinner, my mom and I. It was a beautiful evening with the first promise of summer riding on the breeze, and a sky so clear above us that the stars shone like a million tiny lanterns. We strolled along the Rhône River on our way home, watching the barges glide past, the reflection of their lights stretching across the inky water like shimmering tentacles.

I let my mind wander; I imagined those barges following the river until eventually it emptied into the open sea. How long would it take them to sail from ocean to ocean and finally reach the island I used to call home?

Like before, I was so preoccupied that the man's presence barely registered. He'd been leaning against the stone retaining wall, smoking. Watching us, I know now. As we neared, he pushed away from the wall and dropped his cigarette, grinding it out with the toe of a snakeskin boot. I'm not sure if it was the movement or the boot that drew my attention. All I know is that I was suddenly very aware of him striding toward us.

As I'd been taught, I made a quick catalog of his features without letting my eyes fully rest on his face. He stood a full head taller than me, broad-shouldered but thin almost to the point of being lanky. Even in the darkness, I could see the leathery texture of his skin, like he'd spent a lot of time in the wind and sun. He reminded me of the kind of rugged outdoorsy types they featured in those old Marlboro cigarette ads.

Mom must have felt me stiffen next to her as he neared because she slipped her arm through mine to propel me forward. "Keep walking," she whispered. She didn't have to remind me, though; I knew the drill. *Head up, no eye contact. Just. Act. Casual.*

I patted her hand and laughed as if she'd said something really clever. Okay, so maybe the pat and the laugh were overkill, but I had to do *something* to mask the pounding in my chest and the weird catch in my throat as I drew each breath.

The man brushed past me, so close that the sleeve of his denim shirt touched my arm and I could smell the sharp burnt-roofing-tar stench on his breath. The vibration of his snakeskin boots striking the stones so close to my feet seemed to echo *run, run, RUN!* But even then, I didn't know exactly why.

It took several steps for the dark, smoky stink to register in my head as familiar. And the boots. I'd seen them before. That's when it all came flooding back. That's when I knew.

We'd been found.

To be honest, I was surprised we lasted as long as we did. Despite my very real-looking fake passport and student visa, I had been sure from the moment my mom and I arrived in France that everyone we met must know we were imposters. We kept to ourselves at home and I didn't make friends at school, but no one seemed to notice. I was one of the few students who wasn't boarding there as well and, from the talk I heard in the hallways, they just thought I was a stuck-up American.

By the time we passed the half year mark without incident, I had dared to believe that we might be safe after all. We lived a quiet expat life, me going to a real school instead of taking online classes, and my mom acting like a normal mother instead of a CIA agent. I think we both liked the role-playing reality so much that we wanted it to be true. Little by little, despite the constant training to be vigilant, we began to slip into our faux identities. We began to relax.

Maybe that's why they waited so long to hunt for us. They must have known that once our guard was down, we'd be easier to catch. Exactly who "they" were, I couldn't say, except that they worked for a man called The Mole. He was the leader of a sleeper cell who had turned to organized crime to fund his operation. Both my mom and I had gotten in his way at one point or another, and the man held a grudge.

The Mole and his minions remained faceless to me, which made them all the more terrifying; I never knew who to trust. Plus, I had seen what those minions could do. Twice I had watched people die because of them— first a woman named Bianca on our island back home and then Joe, my mom's CIA partner, in Seattle.

All I could think as the man's footsteps echoed behind me was that the past had caught up with us. It was starting all over again. And I could be next.

Mom's fingers pressed into my skin. "Up," she whispered, steering me toward the stairs that led to street level. We climbed slowly, casually, even as panic swelled in my chest, urging me to move faster.

As we reached the top of the stairs, I could see a night-club about half a block to the left, music and patrons filling the street in front of it. I grabbed my mom and tried to drag her toward the safety of lights and people. It was all I could do not to break into a run, but she held me back.

"What's the matter?" she asked in a low voice. "Who was that man?"

"I don't know who he is but I think he—" My throat constricted, pinching off the words. I had to take a breath and start again. "I think he's following us."

Her brows shot up. "You've seen him before?"

She didn't have to voice the reprimand behind her words; I knew I should have been more aware. I nodded miserably.

She pressed her lips together and nodded. That was enough for the moment, but I knew I would have to explain once it was over. "Let's go."

Even in the balmy night air, my stomach had turned to ice. I focused on the lights of the club and tried not to think about the man behind us. I could feel Mom close behind me and that gave me some comfort, but I still felt as if I had a huge bull's-eye painted between my shoulders.

As we got closer to the club, the music thrummed so loud that I could literally feel the beat. I had to yell to be heard as I pushed my way through the crowd to the open door. *"Pardon. Pardon. Excuse-moi."*

Once inside, I paused to get my bearings. It was one of the rules Mom had drilled into me: *Know where the exits are at all times*. The problem was, the inside of the club was darker than the night outside, with a confusion of colored lights flashing, twirling, pulsing to the music. I could barely make out the silhouette of chairs and tables and people, let alone the layout of the building. A stairway just inside the door led up to a balcony that overlooked the main room of the club, but I knew better than to take the stairs. *Don't escape up.* It wouldn't do us any good to get trapped on a roof with no way down.

Mom pressed close against my back and pointed toward the rear of the club. I squinted through the darkness and relief flooded over me as I spotted a door beyond the bar. An exit. We wound our way around tables and past a crowded dance floor, the dancers jerking like silent film actors underneath the strobe lights.

Suddenly, a man's hand grabbed mine and twirled me onto the floor. I reacted on instinct, all those months of self-defense training with my mom switching into autopilot. I yanked my arm up and out, breaking the hold, while at the same time stomping with my heel as hard as I could. It wasn't until that moment that I realized the man before me was not my pursuer at all, but a much younger guy with brown eyes that widened in surprise—and then pain—as my foot slammed down onto his insole.

"Oh!" I cried. *"Je suis désolée!"* But I didn't have

time for much more of an apology than that. My mom whisked me away before I could do anything else to draw unwanted attention.

I could hear the dancer guy behind us swearing loudly in French, telling anyone who would listen that I was crazy and that all he had wanted to do was dance with me. I didn't have time to feel bad about it. Besides, it was his own fault. He should have asked first.

Still, Mom couldn't resist pressing her cheek close to mine and whispering, "Assess the situation *before* you act!"

"I know," I muttered. "I know."

We reached the back door without further incident and pushed out into a dark alley behind the club. Dirt and age had yellowed the bare bulb above the door so that its weak light barely managed to reach the bottom of the stoop. Shadows swallowed the empty crates and garbage cans beyond. Carefully, we picked our way down the alley to where it intersected the street.

"Now," Mom said, "why don't you tell me what—"

"Shh!" I grabbed her arm and pulled her deeper into the shadows, sniffing the air like a bloodhound. My nose filled with the same raw, burning odor I had noticed when the Marlboro Man passed us by the river. "Do you smell that?"

She frowned. "What?" For a moment I wondered if I had been imagining things, but then her lips parted for a quick intake of breath and her eyes grew wide. "French cigarettes," she whispered. "Cheap ones. Perhaps even hand rolled. Those can be more pungent."

Side by side, we peered around the corner of the building. Sure enough, Marlboro Man stood not more than three feet away from us, sucking on his cheap cigarette, watching the entrance. I was right; he *had* been following us.

"Come on," Mom whispered, and pulled me back down the alley. We slipped down a side street and broke into a full-on run. Looking back, I'm pretty sure my mom had a destination in mind, but all I was thinking about was getting away.

We had gone maybe three or four blocks when Mom slowed to a brisk walk. She scanned the street and then stooped to pick up a loose rock. I thought maybe she was going to try to use it to clobber the Marlboro Man if he came after us, but then we came to a chrome-and-glass phone booth, its flickering fluorescent light casting reverse shadows along the brick sidewalk.

"Keep an eye out," Mom said, and opened the door to the booth. She stepped inside and swung the rock upward, shattering the light.

I jumped at the sound, but I have to admit I was grateful for the resulting cover of darkness.

Inside the booth, Mom picked up the receiver and punched in a number. I inched forward and nudged the edge of the door with my toe so that it wasn't closed all the way. The call connected and I could hear the burr of the phone ringing on the other end of the line. A man's voice answered.

"*C'est moi*," Mom said softly. It's me.

All I heard from the receiver for a long moment was silence, and then the man spoke again. I couldn't make out the words, but there was no mistaking the tone of the voice—low and urgent.

Mom listened quietly and then nodded, as if the man—whoever he was—could see her head move. "*Oui*." She paused again. "*Je comprends*." And then she hung up.

I jumped back as she replaced the receiver, even though I was pretty sure she knew I'd been listening. Before turning to face me, she straightened her sagging posture, and then pushed through the door and started walking. "We have to go."

It took half a second for her words to register. She didn't mean go, as in get away from the phone booth; she meant go, as in clear out. Leave town. Immediately. And, though we had been prepared all along for that eventual probability, I suddenly felt lost.

"Our bags . . ."

"We can't go back for them," Mom said, already walking away. I had to run to keep up with her.

A weight settled on my chest as I realized we were going to abandon the Lyon apartment we had lived in for the past seven months. It's not like we had a lot of memories there, just trappings of our fake lives, but since we'd left everything else behind when we slipped underground, those trappings were all I had. Leaving everything behind was like losing myself all over again.

I started making a mental list of the things I would miss. There wasn't much; we had made a point of not gathering things that could be used to identify us. We kept no journals, took no photos, we didn't have an answering machine because we had no phone. But... my heart sank. We had each kept a small bag with a change of clothes, a little bit of cash and extra copies of our fake identification next to the door in the apartment, in case we needed to leave in a hurry. Even those would be lost. Not that our fake IDs would do us any good now that we'd been found, but it felt like the last thread tying me to the past had been severed.

"What now?" I asked. I hated how small and lost my voice sounded.

Mom didn't even slow her step. "That man on the phone was my contact with the Paris Station. He'll make new arrangements for us."

The CIA's Paris office? I tried not to let my surprise—and concern—show. When we left the States, my mom had taken care of all the details herself because The Mole's minions had infiltrated the Agency and she wasn't sure who she could trust.

My silence must have given away my thoughts,

because she nudged me with her shoulder. "Hey. Don't worry." She tried to sound light and upbeat. "Lévêque will take care of us. We'll meet with him first thing in the morning. Everything will be fine." She gave me a smile that I'm sure was supposed to convey confidence, but after so much time together I was getting to know her too well. I'd come to recognize the little twitch at the corner of her mouth as a sign that she was worried.

She reached for my hand like I was a little kid. "Come, now. The last train to Paris leaves at ten so we'll have to hurry."

Hand in hand we sprinted for the station, arriving out of breath just moments before the train was supposed to leave. The ticket windows were closed so we had to buy our tickets from the machines. It felt like forever that Mom was feeding coins into the slot and another eternity for the machine to print and spit out our tickets. We grabbed them and raced through the turnstile, reaching the train car just as the warning chimes sounded, signaling that the doors were about to close.

The train had already started to move by the time we settled into our seats. I leaned back against the upholstery, silently saying my good-byes to Lyon. Then I noticed Mom's grip on the armrest tighten and I followed her gaze out the window.

Marlboro Man was running onto the platform. Late. Too late. I smiled at his failure . . . until it hit me. My ticket. I flipped it over and my heart dropped. Ours was an express train. No stops between Lyon and Paris. He may have missed us, but he would know exactly where we were headed. And when we would get there.

One glance at Mom and I knew she was thinking the same thing.

We were in trouble.

CHAPTER

2

hugged my arms, eyes darting around the train car like an animal trapped in a moving cage. No, I didn't know for sure that the Marlboro guy worked for The Mole, but it was a pretty safe bet. No one else was looking for my mom and me. No one that I knew about, anyway. So if Marlboro found us, The Mole had found us. The very thought made my insides curdle.

I leaned close to Mom. "Do you think that guy has connections in Paris?" I whispered.

"I don't know."

"But he could."

She looked at me, the expression completely dissolving from her face. "Yes, he could."

I sank back in my seat. That's what I was afraid of. Now that he knew where we were headed, if Marlboro Man had colleagues in Paris, all it would take was a phone call and they could have the station surrounded by the time we got there. Or he could be waiting for us himself. Either scenario made me feel faint.

"Maybe he didn't see us get on the train," I said. But I knew he had; I could tell by the look I'd seen on his face that he knew we'd slipped through his fingers.

Mom didn't answer, but stared straight ahead, tapping her fingers on the armrest. Trying to figure out how we were going to get off the train undetected, I imagined. I hoped she would be able to come up with something, and quickly.

Me, I couldn't think of a thing, which worried me because I was usually pretty good about thinking on my feet. But then again, I hadn't clued in to being followed by the Marlboro guy, had I? It's like when I left my name behind, I lost the thinking part of me as well. I didn't know how to be me, but someone else. I was having an identity crisis, and I'd been running for only seven months. I couldn't imagine how the people who were forever uprooted by the Witness Protection Program maintained their sanity.

As soon as that thought came into my head I tried to push it out again. Because I knew what would follow, and thinking about him hurt too much. "Him" would be Seth Mulo. Seth's family was also on the run from The Mole. The difference was that Seth had been running most of his life.

When he was very young, Seth's parents defected from The Mole's sleeper organization and turned to the U.S. government for asylum. Eventually, the CIA assigned my mom to protect them. She sent Seth and his parents to hide at my dad's island resort where she thought they would be safe. She was wrong. The Mole sent an assassin to kill Seth's parents and naturally, I got caught up in the drama. Together, Seth and I spoiled The Mole's party—which was one of the reasons he wanted us dead.

I stared out at the French countryside, rolling the word *us* around and around in my head. Sadly, with Seth and I, there was no more *us*. We were too dangerous to each other to stay together. The Mole had used me to find Seth in Seattle and I wasn't willing to take the chance again. No, the only solution was for Seth and I to stay far away from each other. That wouldn't stop me from longing for him, though.

Too soon the two-hour ride had passed. I felt the momentum of the train slowing and I had to pull my thoughts from Seth. Lights dotted the landscape, increasing in number as we rolled into the city. We were almost there. I could feel the panic rising like an ice-cold blush.

I tried to act cool, but I'm sure Mom could see the way I was trembling as I turned to her and whispered. "What do we do now?"

She looked at me for a long moment and simply said, "It will be all right." But the corner of her mouth twitched when she said it—and she wasn't even smiling.

The train pulled up to the platform, creaking and groaning to a stop. My stomach twisted. How were we going to get out of the station without getting caught? There weren't many people on the train, so it's not likely we could blend with the crowd. Plus it was after midnight by then, so the station itself wasn't all that crowded. I thought about sneaking out the wrong side of the train and hiding along the tracks, but I was afraid those tracks could be electrified.

"What do we do?" I asked again.

She raised her eyes to meet mine. "I'm going to be sick."

"What?"

She pulled me close and lowered her voice to a whisper. "I'm going to pretend to be sick. Get up and walk toward the exit. I'll be right behind you. Before we get off the train, I'm going to faint. If we're lucky, they'll take us into the station office to make sure I'm all right."

"But . . ." One of the cardinal rules of being on the run was to not draw attention to yourself. Fainting on the train was sure to attract attention. On the other hand, there weren't many people around, so our exposure would be limited. And really? What alternative did we have?

We stood.

"Oh, and one more thing," Mom whispered. "We're French."

At once I understood why she would be the one fainting; Mom and I could both speak French fluently, but my accent was better. When I was just a kid, she had enrolled me in all sorts of language classes because—according to her—I had a gift with languages. She said if you teach a kid a foreign language when they're young enough, they can learn to speak without an accent. The result was that I could speak several languages like a native and a lot more at least conversationally. French was one of the native languages. So I was going to be the mouthpiece. I hoped I was up to it. I straightened. *"Oui, Maman,"* I murmured.

I strolled down the aisle as she said, trying not to look tense as I waited to hear the thud of her dropping to the ground behind me.

I was almost to the door when it happened—only when she fell, it was more like a crash than a thud. Even though I had been expecting her to faint, the noise truly startled me. Which I suppose was good, because when I whirled around to see if she was okay, my reaction was genuine.

"Maman!" I cried. *"Maman!"* She lay sprawled between the seats, her face completely slack. I bent over her and tugged on her hand—as if that would have done any good had she truly fainted. She moaned and rolled her head to the side. I dropped her hand, eyes widening in shock. Something dark and wet matted her hair to the side of her skull. Blood?

The conductor appeared out of nowhere, asking if everything was all right. I turned my eyes to him numbly, not sure what to say. We were supposed to be acting, but the blood was most definitely real. *"Ma mère est blessée,"* I said. It was the truth. My mother was hurt.

He whipped a walkie-talkie from his belt to call for

assistance and then turned his attention back to me. *"Qu'est-ce qui s'est passé?"* he asked. What happened?

Again, I could truthfully say I didn't know. I could guess; she'd probably hit her head when she fell. Beyond that, I wasn't sure. Had she planned it to make her faint seem more convincing?

Another man in a train uniform arrived, carrying a first aid kit. He set it on one of the seats and helped the conductor sit Mom up. She moaned again and blinked her eyes, but held her head fairly steady. I sighed with relief.

"Vous allez bien?" the second guy asked her. Are you all right?

She nodded weakly and allowed him to dab at her head to clean it up. Either she was a really good actress or she was a little dazed to see the amount of blood on the gauze when he pulled it away. I thought she might faint again, for real this time.

Another official-looking person crowded into the aisle behind us. She wore a pinched expression and held a clipboard in her hands. Bingo. Damage control. She would be the one responsible to make sure that the station had no liability for mom's injury.

The gauze guy finished cleaning up the wound, which turned out to be rather small, even though it had bled a lot. He offered to bandage it, but Mom declined. She'd do just as well just holding a compress to her head until it stopped bleeding, she said.

I turned to the clipboard lady and asked if there was someplace my mother could rest.

She was only too willing to comply. *"Absolument,"* she said. Absolutely.

Clipboard Lady showed us into a windowless office crowded with a desk and a couple of chairs. She said that Mom could rest there as long as she needed.

"Merci." I lowered Mom onto one of the chairs. Still holding the gauze pad to her head, she drooped forward until her head rested on the desk.

The lady hovered for a moment. Could she call someone for us? A doctor, perhaps? Did we need anything to eat? To drink? I politely told her no to everything. Mom just needed to rest. Finally, satisfied she had done her duty, the clipboard lady left the room, closing the door behind her.

Mom immediately sat up. "Is she gone?"

I folded my arms. "You scared me half to death."

"Yes, well." She dabbed gingerly at her head. "I didn't quite intend to split my head open, but it was effective, don't you think?"

"Does it hurt?"

"I've had worse. At least the drama gave us a place to hole up for a few hours."

"Hours? When do we meet with whatshisname?"

She threw her bloodied gauze into the trash can. "We won't see him until the café opens at six."

"What café?"

But she was through answering questions. She leaned back in her chair and closed her eyes. "Let's just take advantage of the room while we have it. Get some rest."

Was she kidding? "I'm not tired."

She opened one eye to look at me. "Sleep when you can—" she began, but I finished the mantra for her.

"Because you never know when you might sleep next. I know. But I'm really not tired."

"Suit yourself." She closed her eye again. Soon her breathing fell into a gentle rhythm.

I dropped onto the chair opposite the desk and watched her. It amazed me how she could switch gears like that. Plus, we had no idea if Marlboro or his friends were waiting for us outside the office. How could she be so relaxed? But then again, it *was* late. The more I fought it, the heavier my eyelids became.

The next thing I knew, Mom was shaking my shoulder and whispering my name. "Aphra."

My name, and not the fake one I had been using for the past seven months. For half a heartbeat, I thought I was home and the whole undercover thing had been one long, very bad dream. But then I realized I was still in the station office and reality came flooding back. I shook the sleep from my head. "Time to go?"

She tucked a strand of hair behind my ear. "I'm afraid so."

A quick glance at the clock on the wall told me it was past four. Two more hours until we met Lévêque. I stood. "Let's go."

We hiked to the Metro and rode the night trains all over the city until dawn. I'm afraid I was too tired to get much out of our Paris tour, but I didn't fall asleep again; the Metro wasn't quite as comfortable—or secure—as the office had been. We kept a careful watch out, in case we were being followed, but we never saw anything to make us suspicious. Still, I wasn't convinced that the Marlboro guy would give up so easily.

Finally, just past five-thirty, we got off the Metro at the Louvre-Rivoli station. Even though I knew from the name of the station that we would be next to the Louvre, I wasn't prepared for the wonder I felt as we emerged from the underground to find the museum right in front of us. The sun was about to make its morning debut so the sky was just lightening from purple to mauve, a blushing backdrop for the architecture. The early morning glow reflected softly off the glass pyramid in the courtyard. The effect was quite literally breathtaking.

I forgot all about Marlboro and gawked like a tourist as we walked past the courtyard, beyond the museum and to Tuileries Park, which stretched out behind the Louvre. I had never seen anything like it in my life. I was used to the wild beauty of the island, but the Tuileries was formal, structured, symmetrical. "It's beautiful," I breathed.

"Wait until you see the gardens," Mom said. From the pride in her voice, you'd think she landscaped the place herself. She took me by the hand and led me down the wide paths to the gardens in the center of the park. Standing in the midst of flowers and statues and sculpted shrubberies, I almost believed that we were just sightseeing, until Mom took me by the shoulders and pointed me toward one end of the park.

"Take a moment to orient yourself," she said. "If we get separated, I want you to know where you are."

I nodded, quickly sobered by the thought.

"You see down there?" she continued, pointing. "That is the Obelisk on the Place de la Concorde down the Champs Élysées. At the end of the boulevard there is the Arc de Triomphe. And this way"—she turned me to face in the opposite direction—"is the Carousel. It's like a mini Arc de Triomphe."

"Why do they call it a carousel?"

"Aphra, pay attention. You need to understand the layout of the city in case—"

"We *won't* get separated," I said. She had given me a similar spiel in Lyon, but we'd never been separated there.

"Where we are standing," she continued pointedly, "is the geographic center of the city. There are twenty districts, all laid out in a sort of clockwise spiral from here. We are in district one. If we are ever separated—"

"But we won't—"

She held up her hand to stop me. "If we *are*, I need you to go to Saint-Lazare Station. It's in the eighth district. There is a glass dome in front of the station, and an enclosed phone booth under the dome. That is our meeting place, do you understand?"

I nodded.

"Good." She smiled cheerily. "Now, shall we go get some breakfast?"

I couldn't believe she could think about *food* after all that talk about being separated, but then I quickly remembered. We were meeting Monsieur Lévêque at a café. *"Oui,"* I said quickly. "That sounds good."

I was happy to find that the café in question was a little outdoor restaurant situated right there in the park. We sat at one of the corner tables, facing outward. *Always sit with your back to the wall.*

We had barely settled into our chairs when a tall, elegantly dressed gentleman with a newspaper tucked under his arm took the table right next to ours. He reminded me of the cultured Frenchman in the old *South Pacific* movie Mom and I used to watch back when she lived with my dad and me. He laid his newspaper on the table and summoned the waiter.

"Bonjour monsieur," the waiter greeted him. *"Vous désirez?"*

"Un café serré, s'il vous plait." He ordered his coffee in a very nice baritone voice, and the waiter scurried off.

As the man waited, he unfurled the paper and began

to read. That is, he unfurled *most* of the paper. One section he laid carefully on the table, just at his elbow. His coffee arrived, he sipped delicately for a few moments, then stood and walked briskly away, leaving his newspaper folded neatly on the table.

I was about to comment on the fact when my mom stood abruptly as well. *"Bon. Allons-y,"* she said. Let's go. As she passed the man's table, she swept up the newspaper and tucked it under her arm. Smooth. Natural.

A drop! I couldn't help a flush of pleasure to realize that the cultured Frenchman must be our contact, Lévêque. It was about all I could do to contain myself as Mom and I strolled back through the park toward the Louvre. I was dying to know what was in that newspaper. Our new identities? Money? Instructions?

Finally, Mom motioned to an empty park bench and we sat. She laid the newspaper on the bench beside her. My hands itched with a longing to grab it, open it.

"Aphra," Mom said at length, "how badly do you want to see what's inside that newspaper?"

"Um, very badly?"

"I'm aware of that. Do you know how I know?"

I shook my head.

"The agitation is written all over your face, your body language. If you'd have had the chance, you would have opened the paper long before now, am I correct?"

"I suppose."

"And what do you suppose would have happened

if the paper contained sensitive information? What if someone were watching?"

I stared at her like she was speaking a foreign language.... One I *hadn't* learned.

"You do recall that we were being followed in Lyon, yes? Control is very important, honey. Never let your emotions dictate your actions."

"I understand," I mumbled, feeling about two feet tall.

"Now," she reached for the paper, calmly, slowly. "Let's see what the news has in store for us today."

CHAPTER
3

was disappointed when we found no secret messages folded into the paper. No money, no maps. Nothing I would have expected. But if Mom was similarly let down, she didn't show it. She scanned the print on the front page, as composed as ever. Almost in afterthought, or so it appeared, she handed me the other section of the paper. "Here, why don't you read this one?"

I took the paper, mentally shaking my head. Duh. Our message wasn't folded up inside the paper, it was *in* the paper. Clever. "What am I looking for?" I whispered.

Her eyes never left the page. "We'll know when we find it."

I'm proud to say I was the one who spotted the notation. Actually, it was just a number, written in red ink with a fine, slanted script: *0900*. I found it above an article about Jim Morrison's grave, which lay in a famous cemetery just outside the city.

"This is an interesting article," I said. "Take a look."

She glanced at the paper I held before her and murmured, "Mm-hmm," and then turned back to the section she was reading. I deflated. Maybe the number wasn't significant after all. But then Mom folded her portion of the paper and stood. *"Etes-vous prête à partir?"* Are you ready to go?

I tried not to smile too big. *"Oui, je suis prête."*

We arrived at the cemetery a little bit early. The notation had indicated nine A.M., written in military time. We probably got there around eight-thirty. Even then, we had taken our time getting there; it was only a few miles away from where we'd been. In the end, though, there wasn't a whole lot we could do to waste time that early in the morning.

The sun had barely risen farther in the sky, but the temperature kept climbing. And the humidity. I had watched the clouds gathering overhead and hoped they would cool things down, but they just seemed to hold the moisture in the air.

We wandered through the monuments and gravestones waiting for him, feeling hot and sticky. After having spent the night on the train and slept in the station office without the benefit of a toothbrush or a change of clothes, I was starting to feel pretty rank. All I wanted was to make the contact and go find a nice, cool shower somewhere.

I got half my wish. The clouds dropped lower and then opened up, pouring down rain as if we were standing under a spigot. We ran for the cover of the trees, though we were already soaked through. Then, just as abruptly as it had begun, the rain stopped, though I didn't trust the remaining clouds. Still, no sign of Lévêque.

I was just beginning to think that we had misinterpreted the message when finally I saw him. M. Lévêque, all suave in a designer summer-weight trench coat, strolling along the path toward us. And at least *he* was smart enough to be carrying an umbrella. He stopped just a few headstones down from where we waited and stood, as if paying his respects to the unknown dead. Mom inched nearer to him, but she didn't look in his direction.

"I'm glad to see you're safe," he said in a low voice. His accent was not French.

Mom barely nodded, keeping her eyes downcast.

"Where have you been?" he continued. "You disappeared off the map. Didn't tell anyone where you were, what you were doing . . ."

She bent and straightened the shriveled stems of long-dead roses at her feet. "We were in Lyon," she said simply. "I thought it best we keep to ourselves for a while."

"We can't protect you if we don't know where you are, Natalie."

"I understand. Do you have our new cover?"

"Not yet. There have been some . . . delays."

Her posture went rigid. "What kind of delays?"

"Funding, documents. I'm sorry. We'll meet this afternoon on the running path at the Bois de Boulogne. I hope to have some news for you then." He turned to leave, but called over his shoulder. "I've left you some things with Joan of Arc."

And with that, he strode away. Mom watched him leave, her face completely blank. "Go get the umbrella," she said.

"What umbrella?"

She gestured with her eyes and I followed her gaze to see M. Lévêque pause at the cemetery exit. He folded his umbrella and hung it by its hook handle on the gate as he peeled off his raincoat. He folded the coat neatly over his arm then ambled away from the cemetery without a backward glance.

I ran and grabbed the umbrella, pretending to call out to him in case anyone was watching. *"Monsieur!"* But of course, he kept walking. I tucked the umbrella under my arm. I could feel the crinkle of paper. Money. Or more instructions.

When I returned, Mom was not waiting where I had left her. My first impulse was to run down the path looking for her, but I knew that was irrational. *Don't let your emotions rule your actions,* Mom said. I fought the urge and stayed where I was until she returned, carrying two shopping bags—one in each hand.

"What are—"

"Walk," she said.

I turned and strolled out of the cemetery with her as if it was the most natural thing in the world to have picked up an umbrella and bags in a graveyard.

We didn't open the bags until we were safely checked in to a nearby hotel and locked in our room. Mom looked inside the first bag and threw it to me. "This one's yours," she said.

I opened it like a kid at Christmas. "What is this?" I held up a running shoe.

She pulled out a new pair of running pants and held them against herself for size. "You heard him. We need to meet on the running paths this afternoon."

Whatever. I was just happy to have clean, dry clothes to change into. I tossed aside my soaking-wet Vans and slipped my feet into my new Pumas. They fit perfectly. M. Lévêque was my new best friend.

If only I had known our friendship would turn out to be so short lived.

Since we didn't have to meet M. Lévêque until late that afternoon, Mom mandated that we use some of the time we had to kill by taking a nap. I knew she was big on the rest-when-you-can thing, so I didn't argue, but I knew I wouldn't be able to sleep this time.

I lay on the bed and stared at the ceiling, wondering who I would be in my new life. I doubted we would stay in France; that cover had been blown. I hoped it would be somewhere near the ocean. Somewhere like home. The thought summoned images of my dad back on our island. A deep sadness settled on my chest as it always did when I thought about him. He would be so worried about me. I hoped my note had at least brought him some comfort.

As they often did, my thoughts then drifted back to Seth Mulo. Where was he? Was he still safe? The last time I'd seen him, he was leaving to deliver a ring The Mole wanted in exchange for Seth's dad. I could still feel his arms around me before they came for him. I never even said good-bye; I couldn't make myself form the words. Now I worried that I would never get the chance.

The CIA was supposed to be with Seth on that mission, protecting him, that much I knew, but nothing else. Whenever I asked my mom about him, she would assure me he was safe, but that's about all she would tell me. The last time I asked, she took my hand, but her grip was not gentle and mom-like and comforting. The pressure of her fingers felt like a warning. "We've talked about this," she said evenly. "Seth is safe now. Let him go."

I pulled my hand away. How easy she made it sound. *Let him go.* Like he was some carnival balloon on a string that I could just let loose and forget once he had floated away.

She didn't understand.

Seth and I shared a bond that Mom with all her agent smarts should have anticipated when she sent him to our island. He was sensitive and smart and made me feel special when I was with him. And more than that, we understood each other. We had been through hell and back together. How could she ask me to turn my back on that?

A familiar ache swelled in my throat, and my chest felt at once heavy and hollow. I didn't want to admit it, but maybe my mom was right. Seth was gone. For his safety, as well as our own, I could never see him again. Thinking about him all the time was like slow torture. Whether I liked it or not, I had to let go of his memory.

I pushed off of the bed and padded into the bathroom, where I took a long, hot shower, washed my hair, and had a good, long cry. I hoped that it would get easier as time went by.

Mom woke when I came out of the bathroom and headed in for a shower of her own. By the time we were both dressed in our new clothes, my stomach was starting to growl. We hadn't eaten since dinner the night before and that seemed like a long, long time ago.

I sat at the desk, thumbing through the guest services book the hotel had left in our room. "Can we order room service?" I asked. "I'm starving."

Mom paused from combing out her wet hair. "I saw a patisserie on the corner this morning. Why don't we go grab something?"

"Is that okay?"

She picked up the room card and the roll of euros

Lévêque had left for us and stuffed them both in her pocket. "Sure. We can cut through the hotel lobby to minimize exposure."

I tossed the amenities book aside and bounced off the bed. "How long until we have to meet at the park?"

"Not until after he gets off work at five. Another couple of hours. We have time." She opened the door and stepped aside. "After you."

I was feeling a little better since my cry in the shower. Not much, but a little. I wondered if it showed, this monumental decision I'd made. Would Mom notice? I caught a glimpse of myself in the elevator mirror as we rode down to the lobby. As far as I could see, I looked exactly the same—only in more expensive clothes. You know, the kind that real athletes wear: a layered racer tank and matching shorts, both made from that lightweight fabric that's supposed to wick the moisture away from your skin. At least that was different. I suppose that was the best I could expect.

In the lobby, we had just started walking to the door when the desk clerk called after Mom.

"Pardon, Madame." He waved an envelope at her. "Il y a un message pour vous."

The smile froze on her face. She thanked him, and accepted the message with about as much enthusiasm as she might have taken a vial of toxin. She turned it over to read the front and that little muscle at the side of her lips started twitching again.

"*Quand est-il arrivé?*" she asked. When did it arrive?

The clerk started speaking rapid-fire French, apologizing like he thought he was in trouble. He said that he had just begun his shift a short time ago and didn't know when it had arrived, only that it was there when he got in. "*Je ne sais pas,*" he kept saying, "*je ne sais pas.*"

Mom managed a smile and thanked the clerk, assuring him that all was well. But I could tell she was shaken. She tucked the envelope into her pocket and suggested we use the restroom before we left for our day about town. If I hadn't already guessed something was up, I knew then; we weren't headed "about town." We were just going to the patisserie next door. We detoured to the ladies' room, where she locked the door and leaned up against it. Gingerly, she tore open the envelope and read the note inside. For the first time I could remember, she let her blank facade slip. Her eyes grew wide and her lips turned down, parting just enough to draw in a gasp. She stole a quick glance at her watch.

"What is it?" I asked.

"I need to go. Alone." She pushed the door open to one of the stalls and started ripping the note into tiny pieces, letting them drop into the toilet. "Do you remember our meeting place?"

I stared at her. "I don't understand. Isn't that only for if we became separated?"

"We will be. But only for a short while." She flushed

the note away and turned to face me, but she couldn't meet my eyes. My stomach felt hollow. This was not my usual in-control mom.

"What is it?"

She just shook her head and raked her fingers through her still-damp hair. I couldn't help but notice the way her fingers were trembling. That's when I got really scared.

"Mom . . ."

She grasped my hand. "Wait for me at the phone booth under the glass dome at the Saint-Lazare station. And if you don't see me within—"

"I'm coming with you."

She shook her head. "Not this time."

"Why? What's wrong, Mom?"

"Aphra, I need to ask you to trust me on this. I'll tell you eveything as soon as I can, but now is not the time. I'm sorry."

"How long will you be?"

Ignoring my question, she pulled the money from her pocket and peeled off four large bills. "Put these away. Wait for me at Saint-Lazare. If I am not there in two hours, go to the U.S. consulate."

I was genuinely scared by then. "What's going on? What was in that note?"

Finally, Mom gave in. "It was from Gérard Lévêque," she said in a low voice. "He says we must leave Paris immediately. I'm to meet him for instructions." She kissed me on the forehead. "Wait for me at Saint-Lazare. I love you."

And then she was gone.

If ever I needed a signal that she still thought of me as her little girl, that kiss was it. And as much as the gesture made me feel all warm and fuzzy inside, I didn't want her to see me as a helpless little girl just then. I needed her to believe in me. Maybe that's why I chose to do what I did.

I waited for a few seconds and then eased out of the ladies' room to follow her. I know I had promised that I would wait at Saint-Lazare, but I couldn't leave her. Like she said that morning, when a person lets her emotions think for her, that's when she gets into trouble. Well, the way she had reacted, I knew the note had evoked an emotional response that wasn't allowing her to think rationally.

The desk clerk barely glanced up as I ran from the lobby, which was a good thing because I'm sure my face would have betrayed too much. I tried to hide the worry as I jogged down the street toward the Metro, but I'm not sure I succeeded.

I hid behind the station sign, watching my mom pace up and down the platform, waiting for the train. I felt naked. Exposed. Because I could think of only one reason Lévêque would warn us to leave Paris. The Mole had found us again.

When the train arrived, I slipped onto the car next

to the one my mom took. I positioned myself behind a large man in a *Les Bleus* T-shirt and watched her through the sliding door.

Every time we made a stop and more people pushed on board, my chest grew tighter and tighter until I could barely breathe. And each time the doors slid closed, it felt like a snare snapping shut, over and over again.

Mom got off the train at the Esplanade de la Défense station. She jogged along a gravel path that followed the contours of the Seine until she had to stop for traffic at the intersection of a large bridge. On the other side of the bridge stretched a huge wooded park.

I ducked and hid in the bushes along the path until the route was clear, and then eased out into the foot traffic, following her down a wide path that led through the trees.

If she hadn't been distracted, there's no way I could have gotten away with following her without her knowing. It just served as further proof that she was not herself. She *needed* me.

As parks go, the one I followed her through that day was beyond beautiful. The running path wound past lakes and miniature waterfalls, and was canopied by tall oak trees that must have been hundreds of years old. Sometime in its history, the park must have been part of an estate; an elegant mansion stood at one end of the property, surrounded by an ornate fence. I imagined the running paths had once been meant for horses.

I kept a close eye on my mom's bouncing head several strides ahead of me, pulling farther and farther ahead with every step. She wasn't jogging; she was flat-out running. It would have been easier to keep up with her if the park wasn't such a popular destination. The track was clogged with runners and cyclists and people simply out for a lovely summer stroll. Of course, I'm sure that's why Lévêque had chosen that particular park to meet. Among the throngs of other joggers, they would practically be invisible as they ran side by side, sharing information. But it made it harder for me to keep my distance, still keeping her in sight without being obvious about it.

When we rounded a curve in the path, I had to slow for a woman with a jogging stroller and then again for some guy running with his dog. A group of older men were walking four abreast, and I had to slow my stride again to wait for an opening so I could get past them. Still, I managed to keep pace.

But then a group of little kids dressed in matching outfits ambled onto the path, herded by a pinched-faced teacher. Boys and girls alike wore crisp, white tunics over navy blue shorts, with round straw hats on their heads that had little ribbons dangling down the back. They were cute, but in my way. When I slowed down to avoid running them over, Mom pulled even farther ahead. I veered to the left of the group and tried to pass them, but one little boy dropped the toy boat he was carrying and stooped right in front of me to pick it up.

I stumbled to a stop. The teacher jumped forward to pull him out of my way, gushing apologies. *"Pardon, mademoiselle! Désolé."*

"Ne t'en fais pas," I murmured. It's okay. But it wasn't quite, because when I looked up, my mom was gone. I flew down the path, feeling like that little kindergartner again. Only this time it was worse because my mind slipped back to the last time I had lost my mom in a crowd. That incident had ended with me watching her partner die.

The logical part of my brain knew it was highly unlikely for the same thing to happen again. Still, I half expected to round the bend and find M. Lévêque sitting at one of the park's small, round tables, reading his newspaper, reaching for his coffee the way her partner, Joe, had done . . . right before he keeled over from being poisoned.

I shook my head to chase the thought away. The only thing I needed to be worried about was finding my mom. It seemed unreal to me that I could have lost her so quickly. I had been distracted for only a moment.

And then her voice echoed in my head, so urgent, reminding me to go to the station.

I drew in a shaky breath, a weight settling on my chest. Maybe I wasn't so sneaky after all. She had probably seen me following her and ditched me. But why? What was it about this meeting that was so different from this morning? I thought of how she had been so shaken when she read the note. This meeting with M. Lévêque must be dangerous if she didn't want me there, but if it was too dangerous for me, it would be just as dangerous for her.

Suddenly, I was unsure of what to do. Should I try to find her? She might need help. I started down the path again, but stopped before I had gone three steps. I could just imagine what she would say if I went against following the procedure she had taken such pains to spell out to me. Especially if by doing so, I messed up whatever it was she was planning. She had made it very clear she wanted me to go to the station and wait for her there.

Mom had always said to trust my instincts . . . but what if my instincts told me two completely different things?

In the end, I decided to go to Saint-Lazare as I had promised. She had made it clear that she didn't want me with her. I slogged back to the Metro, defeated. On the map outside the gate, I was able to find Gare Saint-Lazare and determine the route I should go. I pulled one of the bills from my pocket and bought a ticket, slipping through the turnstile before I could change my mind.

The platform was crowded with commuters in suits and ties, parents with fidgeting children, tourist-types in Bermuda shorts thumbing through guidebooks, and what looked like an entire rugby team. They were all talking, laughing, acting as though it were any other normal day. I tried to blend in with them, but I'm not sure how well I succeeded in adapting their casual postures and worry-free expressions.

From down the track, I could see the headlights of the train approaching. I stole one last glance back toward the park, half hoping to see Mom jogging toward the Metro. That's when I saw him. He was standing at the entrance to the Metro, smoking one of his foul cigarettes. The Marlboro Man. My breath caught. It couldn't be a coincidence. Could it?

Just then, he turned his head and looked toward the platform. I jumped behind one of the support pillars, heart hammering. I didn't know if he saw me, but I wasn't going to wait to find out.

A train rolled to a stop on the tracks behind me and the doors opened with a hydraulic hiss. I jumped into the crowd of commuters and pushed my way onto the nearest car. When I looked back at where he had been standing, I couldn't see him anymore. Where had he gone?

And why wasn't the train moving? Cold sweat prickled across the back of my neck. Any second, I expected to see Marlboro stroll up onto the platform and corner me on the train. I looked around frantically, searching for an alternate exit.

Fortunately, I didn't need it. The doors slid shut and the train began to move. I gripped the handrail to keep my balance and leaned against the door, resting my forehead on the cool glass as I watched the station slip away.

As the train picked up speed I studied the route map on the LED display above the door. There were eight stops before I had to transfer trains at the Champs Élysées station. Only two more stops from there to Saint-Lazare. If I figured an average of about three minutes between stops, that meant at least half an hour before I reached our meeting place. Half an hour that my mom could be in trouble.

But I tried not to think about that. I tried not to think about anything as the train rolled through station after station. People got off, more people got on. I avoided looking at any of them directly. I felt like I had a huge neon sign above my head flashing the words *Scared American*.

Located as it was in the heart of the city, the station at Champs Élysées was much more crowded than the one at la Défense had been. I'm not really used to crowds. Logically, I knew that it should be easier to lose myself in the mob at the station, but it only made me feel more conspicuous. And as I searched for the right track for the train to Saint-Lazare, I couldn't shake the feeling that I was being watched. I spun around, fully expecting to find Marlboro Man lurking in one of the corners.

My mom would have been disappointed if she could have seen my lack of cool. My first time away from her in Paris and I was completely falling apart. I forced a deep breath—not the best idea in a Paris Metro station, believe me—and tried to release some of the tension as I blew it out again. It didn't work. The best I could manage was to keep my face blank and try to blend in by walking to the next track like I had some kind of purpose.

Before I got to the platform, a garbled French voice announced over the loudspeaker the arrival of the train. At least that's what I think it said. It was too distorted to understand, but I could see *something* approaching, so I ran to meet it.

It wasn't until the train pulled up to the platform that I was able to read the destination sign by the train's sliding doors. It wasn't the one I wanted. I glanced up at the huge digital board on the wall to look for line thirteen. It took me a moment to find it. Which might be why I didn't see him step up behind me.

He touched my arm. "Excuse me."

Automatically, my head whipped around—not only because he spoke in English when I would have expected French, but because I recognized the voice. I could quite literally feel the blood drain from my face, and it felt like it had been replaced by ice water.

"Ryan?" I managed to whisper. I'd last seen CIA Agent Ryan Anderson in the Cascades in Washington State. What was he doing in Paris? Did it have anything to do with my mom's meeting with Lévêque in the park? I began to open my mouth, but he shook his head just enough to signal me that I should hold my tongue.

What came next happened so suddenly that even now as I look back, it catches me by surprise. The chimes on the platform gave the closing-door warning. Just before they slid shut, Ryan grabbed my arm and dragged me onto the train.

"I'm sorry," he said, "but there's been a change of plans."

CHAPTER
4

tried to wrench away from him, but Ryan kept a firm grip on my arm, just above the elbow. I don't know if he intended it or not, but his thumb hit a pressure point when he squeezed and it really hurt.

On a seat nearby, a gray-haired gentleman with horn-rim glasses lowered the paper he was reading to give me a questioning look. He raised his brows as if to ask if I was all right. For a very brief moment, I considered shouting that I was not, in fact, all right, but then my mom's words swirled through my head. *Assess the situation. Act, don't react.*

I didn't know why Ryan was there. I didn't know how he had found me. Most of all, I didn't know if he had anything to do with my mom's disappearance in the park. The one thing I *did* know was that until I knew the answers to those questions, it would be better for me to keep my mouth shut.

I gave the man what I hoped was a reassuring smile—one that would not only convey my appreciation for his concern, but would give him confidence that I was in control of the situation. Only I wasn't. In control, I mean. My legs shook so badly that I very nearly sank to the floor. I had to bite my tongue to hold back the questions threatening to tumble out of my mouth.

I stole a glance at Ryan's face. Like my mom, he had the annoying ability to maintain a completely blank expression. But his eyes . . . I dropped my gaze quickly. The warm velvet brown of his eyes might have made me feel protected and safe . . . except for the fact that he had found me in Paris, where my mom and I were supposed to be completely incognito.

The man with the newspaper seemed to sense my unease and gave me one last grandfatherly glance. For his benefit and to preserve the illusion I was trying to create, I leaned into Ryan and rested my head on his shoulder. That must have taken Ryan completely by surprise because he flinched, muscles tensing before he caught himself and forced them to relax. The man didn't seem to notice the reaction, though. He went back to his newspaper, apparently satisfied that all was well.

The train slowed, and I stumbled forward. Ryan caught me with one arm and set me back on my feet. It was my turn to flinch, because he didn't let go of me after I'd recovered, but pulled me closer. He brushed my hair back from my ear and leaned in close so that his head nearly touched mine.

"This is our stop," he whispered. His warm breath feathered against my neck, a not unpleasant sensation, I had to admit. He straightened as the train rolled to a stop and let his arm slide down so that his hand rested firmly at the small of my back. Not in a romantic way, but not really detached, either, just kind of . . . protective.

The doors slid open and he guided me forward. Once we were off the train, he grabbed my hand and picked up the pace as he pulled me through the crowd. I realized too late that I had forgotten rule number one. I hadn't been paying attention to the route on the train and I didn't recognize the platform we were on at all—the layout and posters on the curving wall didn't seem familiar. I twisted my head around to see the station sign, but it didn't do me any good; I didn't recognize the name. I had no idea where we were.

Near the exit gate, the crowd knotted and snarled before feeding through the cage-like revolving door turnstile one by one. Ryan's grip on my hand tightened and I noticed the way his jaw tensed and flexed. I could guess what he was thinking: Only one of us could go through the turnstile at a time. If I went through first, I could bolt the moment I got to the other side. If he went through first, I could turn around and run the other way. But neither scenario would do me much good.

I gave his hand a squeeze to let him know I wasn't going anywhere. I still didn't know what was going on, but my gut told me that Ryan was on my side, even if I didn't always agree with his methods. Besides, I was smart enough to realize that if I took off as soon as he released me, he'd only come after me. A chase through

the subway was not the best plan for keeping a low profile. Plus, where would I run *to*? I didn't know the area.
He had nothing to worry about. Yet.

Ryan let go of my hand when we reached street level
and slipped his arm around my waist. He leaned close
again. "Try to look a little less miserable," he said in a low
voice. "People are beginning to stare."

"Why don't you tell me what's going on," I whispered
back, "and then maybe I'll *be* a little less miserable."

He smiled at that, but whether it was real or for show,
I hadn't the slightest idea.

I tried to get my bearings as we walked. Judging from
the boutiques and small cafés, we were in one of the older
quarters, but I hadn't been in Paris long enough to know
which one. Buildings with ornate detailing sprouted up
directly from the narrow cobblestone streets—no side-
walks, no landscaping. The streets themselves wound
and curved until I was completely turned around. Of
course, maybe that's what Ryan was counting on.

Finally, he stopped in front of the recessed entryway
of one of the buildings. He gave me a quick once-over
and then said, "Keep your head down."

I did as I was told, but not before sneaking a quick peek
at the entry in question. As with the windows above, the
door was framed by elaborate molding that arched dra-
matically across the top. Along the right side of the door
was a call box with a row of black buttons labeled with

gold numbers. Above the box, a security camera pointed downward, presumably so that apartment owners could see who was ringing before they let them in. Which would be why Ryan wanted me to lower my head.

The door buzzed and Ryan opened it. He stood to the side and nodded toward the interior. "After you."

Cast in shadow, the hallway inside looked like a prison cell. I hesitated.

"Aphra," Ryan said. It sounded like a warning.

I stood my ground. "No. Not until you tell me what's going on."

For an instant a shadow passed over his face, just before the blank expression took over again. "We'll talk about it inside, you have my word." He swept a quick glance up the street. "Not here."

"I just want to know what's—"

Before I could react, his hand whipped out and grabbed my arm. He dragged me forward until our faces were literally centimeters from each other. This time, the sensation I got from his close proximity was far from pleasant. "Natalie is waiting for you," he said through gritted teeth.

Why hadn't he said so in the first place? A rush of relief swept over me and I allowed him to pull me inside. The door slammed heavily behind us.

The building didn't have an elevator so we took the stairs. It was only a couple of flights up, Ryan told me as we climbed.

"We're borrowing an apartment," he explained. "Very temporarily."

I nodded grimly, remembering how Mom and her partners had been "subletting" her place back in Seattle. Not for the first time, I wondered what happened to the owners when the Agency needed a place to set up shop.

In the hallway upstairs, cooking smells mingled with old-building mustiness and stale cigarette smoke. Ryan led the way down a long hallway lined on either side by dark, narrow doors. It was eerily silent except for a faint baby's cry and the distant sound of someone practicing an intricate run on a piano. We stopped at a door with a brass 29 tacked beneath a matching peephole.

Ryan gave the door three sharp knocks, paused, and then knocked twice more. From inside came the sound of hurried footsteps and then the metallic click of locks being drawn.

The door cracked open an inch or two and then closed again. Another metallic sound—a security chain, I guessed—and then the door swung open. To my disappointment, it wasn't my mom who stood there, but a tall redheaded woman in a stark black business-type suit. The look on her face was far from welcoming, but she motioned us inside, anyway.

"What took so long?" she snapped as she reset the series of locks on the door.

"She'd already gotten on the train," Ryan said.

"Where's my mom?" I asked.

"Aphra?"

I spun to find Mom crowding into the small entryway. She reached out for me and gathered me into her arms, holding me so tightly that I could barely breathe.

When she let me go, I turned to Ryan. "Now will you please tell me what's going on?"

He exchanged a meaningful look with the red-haired lady. "I think we'd better sit down," he said.

The redhead ushered us all into a tiny kitchen equipped with the smallest appliances I'd ever seen. Seriously. You couldn't even fit a cookie sheet into the oven and the fridge looked like one of those little cube things you might put in a dorm room. The stainless-steel sink was about the size of something you'd find on an airplane, complete with a leaky faucet.

We settled onto uncomfortable metal filigree chairs around a small glass-topped table. Ryan clasped his hands as if he was about to pray and rested them on the table in front of him. He took a deep breath and inclined his head toward the redhead.

"This is Agent Janine Caraday." He spoke directly to me. I supposed the introductions had already been made to my mom. "She works with the Paris Station."

I nodded, confused. I thought no one at the Paris Station besides Lévêque knew we were there.

"She was hoping you and your mom could be of some assistance."

"With what, exactly?"

"Lévêque sent me a message this morning," Caraday said. "He arranged a meeting, but then he never showed."

I looked to my mom, frowning. How much were we supposed to let on and to whom? "Lévêque? I'm not sure I—"

"Your mother has already confirmed that he was your contact," Caraday cut in.

Was? I didn't like the sound of that. "What happened? Where is he?"

Ryan answered, almost apologetically. "Lévêque is dead."

I felt like a hole opened beneath my chair. The blackness sucked and pulled at me. I flicked a look at Mom, and the grief on her face told me that she had accepted the news. I didn't. I couldn't. "What? No. He can't be. He was . . . He wanted to meet with us. We just got his note and—"

Mom held up her hand to silence me and asked in a soft voice, "How did it happen? When?"

"They found him in the river this morning," Ryan said.

The room tilted and I grasped the table for balance. We had just *been* with Lévêque that morning. He must have been killed right after he left us. I thought back to my premonition in the park and imagined Lévêque once again, sitting at a quiet table, sipping his coffee. This couldn't be happening. Not again.

"We need your help," Agent Caraday said.

It was a little late for help. At least for Lévêque. Besides, what could we possibly do? They already seemed to know more than we did.

"We believe his death is connected to his contact with you," she continued. "He . . ." Her voice broke and she let her gaze stray to the window. She pressed her lips together. Hard. Finally, she spoke again. "Forgive me. Gérard Lévêque was a friend."

"I'm very sorry," my mom said gently. "He was a good man."

"Yes, he was," Caraday's voice wasn't soft and mournful anymore. She practically bit off each word.

Mom leaned forward, laying her hands on the table. "He sent an urgent note to the hotel this morning, asking me to meet him. I didn't receive the note for several hours after it arrived. And now . . ." Her words trailed off and it took her a moment to find them again. "What can we do to help?"

Caraday didn't hesitate. She stood and retrieved a boxy leather attaché case and brought it to the table. From the case, she withdrew three plastic evidence bags and laid them on the glass.

"These were found on his body." She pushed forward a bag that contained deep blue strips of cloth that showed white in the frayed edges. Denim. "His hands and feet were bound with this. The same fabric was used as a gag."

I stared at the bag, my stomach turning. The edges of the plastic were foggy with condensation. The denim was still wet. They must have collected the samples right after they pulled him from the river.

And it was about to get worse.

Caraday picked up another bag and removed about a dozen Polaroid photos. She fanned them onto the table and selected one that showed a close-up of a man's wrist. The skin was gray except for a shadowed ribbon of purple punctuated by claret-colored scrapes. "These ligature marks indicate signs of struggle. Notice how the skin is rubbed raw here and here."

She tapped the photo to indicate where we were supposed to look, but I couldn't make myself focus on the picture at all.

"Here you will see the image from a computed tomography that shows sediment in his paranasal sinuses. We also found frothy liquid in his airway and fluid in his ears, all indicative of drowning."

That meant Lévêque had been alive when his killer threw him into the river. Bile rose in my throat and I had to swallow hard to keep it down.

"You can see indications of struggle here," she continued, pulling out a partial headshot of Lévêque, only you wouldn't know it was him because the face was all puffy and ashen and the mouth was distorted, pulled into a perpetual grimace by a band of cloth stretched tight like a horse's bit. "It appears he tried to bite through the cloth, but was unsuccessful. At first we assumed that the gag was simply that, a gag, but when we removed it, we found this."

She slid the third baggie forward. It contained another piece of cloth, this one white—perhaps a handkerchief. Someone had written on it with black marker. "We're hoping you can tell us what it means."

My mom glanced up. "What is it?"

"A note we found stuffed in his mouth," Caraday said matter-of-factly.

I could feel the blood drain from my face as my head went light.

Ryan slid a worried look to Caraday. "Maybe we shouldn't do this with her in the room."

His concern comforted and riled me at the same time. I wasn't a baby. I had seen the effects of murder before. But this . . . I couldn't shake the awful feeling that Lévêque had died solely because he had met with us that morning. Otherwise, why would Caraday be talking to us?

Ryan gave me what I thought was an encouraging nod. "If you want to wait in the other room . . ."

"No. I'm fine. Thanks." I straightened in my seat, mimicking Caraday's detachment. "What does the note say?" My voice shook only a little.

Caraday smoothed the edges of the plastic bag and read aloud: "*The fourth will find where they hide deliver the children lest he should ride 07060800.*"

I scrunched my brows in confusion. "What does it mean?"

Ryan shifted on his chair and looked to my mom. "We were hoping you could tell us."

I glanced at Mom. She was studying the note with a perplexed look on her face.

"Clearly the note is a warning meant for you," Caraday said impatiently. "You notice that Lévêque was not killed near his home or workplace, but near the park where you were supposed to meet."

"I don't understand. . . ." Mom said.

"Someone knew your plans! And they wanted us to know they knew. Every detail of the murder was planned to send a message. We even ran tests on the fabric. Vintage Italian denim. *Cimosati* selvedge. Used in the Parades collection last season."

"Where was it manufactured?" The strain in Mom's voice caught my attention. I turned to stare at her. Though her face revealed nothing, her hands were clasped so tightly together in her lap that her knuckles were turning white.

Caraday didn't miss a beat. "Northern Italy. Lombardy region. Lakeside town by the name of Varese, just north of Milan. But the mill's been closed for years."

Mom closed her eyes for a long moment and drew a deep breath before speaking. "I know what the note means."

CHAPTER
5

We all sat silent; the only sound in the room was the steady *drip, drip, drip* of the leaky faucet. Mom stood up and broke away from the table, pacing across the room. She turned to face us. "The Mulo family have recently . . . relocated to Varese," she said, her voice hollow.

I blinked at her, not wanting to comprehend the significance of that statement. If every detail of Lévêque's murder had been planned to send a message, then using fabric made in the very city where the Mulos were hiding meant only one thing. They, also, had been found.

Caraday nodded slowly, turning the new information over in her head. She watched my mom with interest. "What do you make of the note?"

"Nothing that you haven't already thought of, I'm sure."

"Perhaps," Caraday said, "but I'd like to hear your interpretation."

Mom folded her arms and shrugged. "'The fourth' refers to the fourth horseman of the apocalypse, as described in the Book of Revelation. 'I looked and there before was a pale horse,'" she quoted. "'Its rider was named Death.'"

A shiver passed through me at those words, but Caraday only nodded. "And the numbers?"

"The numbers indicate a date and time. July sixth at 0800 military time—eight o'clock in the morning. Our deadline, perhaps."

"Who are 'the children'?"

I didn't want to hear the words, because I knew exactly who the children were, but it didn't stop me from holding my breath as I waited for Mom's answer.

"My daughter," Mom said miserably, "and the Mulos' son, Seth."

"What does it mean, 'deliver the children'?" Ryan asked. "Deliver them from death?"

"I don't think it means *deliver* in the biblical sense," Mom said, her voice dead. "It means *deliver them*, as in give them up."

"So a threat is implied," Caraday mused.

I snorted. *"Implied?"*

Her expression didn't change. "He wants Aphra and Seth."

"He?" I asked. "You know who did this?"

Caraday and Ryan exchanged a look. Sort of a how-much-do-we-tell-the-kid kind of thing that made my blood boil.

"Tell me," I demanded, although I was afraid I already knew the answer.

"Aphra," Mom said, shaking her head. I could see on her face that she knew the answer, too.

"No. I want to hear it."

Caraday cleared her throat. "We had wondered if The Mole was involved, and now . . . Well, this has confirmed our fears. It makes perfect sense."

"No," I shot back. "It makes no sense at all. If The Mole knew where my mom and I were, why did he have to kill Lévêque? Why not just come after us? And what's with the note? If he knows where the Mulos are, what does he need us for?"

"He *doesn't* know where the Mulos are," Caraday said. "Our intelligence sources tell us that he is still searching. He has identified the city, but so far the Mulos have managed to stay hidden. Even our operatives haven't been able to find them."

Mom bristled. "You have people *looking* for them?"

"For protection only," Caraday soothed. "Once we discovered that The Mole was gathering his forces, we knew he must be closing in."

"So he's baiting us," Mom murmured, sinking back onto the chair. "He wants us to lead him to the Mulos."

"No," Caraday said, "He wants *your daughter* to lead him to the Mulos."

Mom flinched, but she didn't deny it.

"Why me?" I asked.

Caraday shrugged. "The Mole has a psychopathic profile. No remorse. No conscience. Manipulative. Callous. Pathologically egocentric. You and the Mulo boy have vexed him ever since you captured his assassin on your island."

I closed my eyes, trying to blot out the memory. A Japanese assassin named Hisako had followed Seth's family to our island. She was the one who had killed Bianca. She had nearly killed my dad. Seth and I were only doing what we had to do to protect our families. Besides, Hisako had come after us, not the other way around.

"We . . . didn't mean to 'vex' anyone," I said weakly.

"Add to that the insult of unmasking his two top men within the Agency," Caraday continued, "and he wants more than just revenge. He wants satisfaction."

I felt like a giant hand had closed around my chest. I couldn't breathe. The Mole wanted Seth and me dead. And then he would kill Seth's family. And probably my mom. The hand squeezed. I'd seen what The Mole could do . . . or rather, what his minions could do. And although I had known since the showdown with his henchmen in the Cascades that I was on his hit list, it had never seemed completely real to me. Not even while Mom and I floated around France, as invisible as ghosts. But now I knew he knew where I was and suddenly it became very real. Undeniably so.

But why give us a month's warning?

Then it struck me. "Wait! You got the date wrong."

"What?"

"The dates. You said 0706, right? They write the day first here, not the month."

Caraday's eyes widened. "Of course. He didn't mean July sixth, he meant June seventh."

"What day is it?" I asked.

"June sixth," Ryan said.

Cold fear snaked down my back. I turned to my mom. "Do the Mulos have a phone? Can we call them?"

She shook her head. "No phones," she said quietly. "Too dangerous."

"Then we have to go warn them!"

"I'm glad to hear you say that"—Caraday leaned across the table and took my hand—"because we have a plan that will help us do just that."

My brows slid downward. "You already have a plan? But you just found out where—"

She waved my question away. "As soon as we ran the tests on the fabric, we knew that Varese was significant. A signal. And now"—she nodded to my mom—"we understand why. Our suspicion has been confirmed. A special team has been gathering, ready for my word. With you on board—"

Mom drew an indignant breath. "You're not suggesting that *Aphra* go to Varese!"

Caraday leaned back in her chair. "That's exactly what I'm suggesting. The Mole won't be able to resist. And as soon as he reveals himself—" She slammed her hand onto the table.

"Oh, no. You will not use my daughter as bait."

"She'll be safe." She fixed my mom with a challenging look. "Just as safe as young Mulo was when you dangled him in front of The Mole's men in Cardiff."

"What?" I looked from Caraday to my mom. "What is she talking about?"

Mom shook her head. "Nothing. It doesn't have anything to do with—"

"Your mother," Caraday interrupted, "instructed Seth Mulo to draw his father's captors from the house when he delivered that ring so that the Agency could capture them. Sounds like bait to me."

I leaned away from my mom. "You *what*?"

"I wasn't in charge of the operation," she protested.

"But you are the one the boy trusted. You told him what to do," Caraday insisted.

I turned to my mom. "Tell me. What happened when Seth returned the ring?"

She didn't speak for a long moment.

"I can tell you," Caraday said.

"No, I will." Mom shifted in her seat. "When Joe found the ring," she said, speaking of her dead partner in Seattle, "he had it scanned to retrieve the list of names etched into the stone. That's how he was able to identify Stuart as a member of The Mole's cell." Stuart had been her other partner, a double agent. I could see the hurt of his betrayal still in her eyes. He had nearly killed us both. In that moment, I understood her reluctance to tell me what I wanted to know. She was trying to protect me. What she didn't understand was that not knowing what had happened to Seth hurt worse than anything The Mole or any of his minions could do to me.

"So what happened then?" I prodded.

"We couldn't let them know we had discovered the secret of the ring; it was the only reason they were keeping Victor Mulo alive—as a trade to get the ring back. But we knew, based on their track record, that they would probably kill him once they had the ring, so we had to take steps to prevent that."

"It would have been an awful death," Caraday put in. "He had crossed his former comrades. They have a special hatred for traitors."

Mom shot her a withering look and Ryan coughed. "A little too much information," he said.

Caraday slid him a sideways glance. "She's old enough to handle the truth, don't you think? She's seen enough of it already."

She was right. I folded my arms and looked back to Mom. "What did you do to prevent it?"

"We knew that they would consider it a coup to kill two Mulos, so . . ." She ran her hand through her hair. "We did arrange for Seth to make the drop. But he was heavily covered. We knew they would come after him, and we were ready when they did. He wasn't harmed at all."

I stared at her, seeing her in a much different light.

She looked like a complete stranger to me. "I can't believe you'd allow that. I thought your job was to *protect* Seth and his family."

"He *was* protected." She reached for my hand but I pulled it away. "An entire team of highly trained specialists were with him."

"Just like a team will be with Aphra when she goes to Varese," Caraday said.

"She's not *going* to Varese," my mom shot back.

I pushed away from the table. "Stop. Just, stop!" I ran from the kitchen but the apartment was so small I didn't really have anywhere to go. I paced in the tiny front room, ready to burst.

I heard a chair scrape against the kitchen floor and then Caraday's voice said, "I'm sorry. I shouldn't have dropped this on you like that. I should apologize to your daughter."

I folded my arms and waited for her to appear in the doorway.

She entered the living room tentatively. "This has been a lot for one day, hasn't it?"

I raised my chin. "You think?"

She took a step toward me. "Look, Aphra. I'm sorry. I know this isn't easy for you."

That was putting it mildly.

"You have to understand, I—"

"You were right."

She threw a quick glance over her shoulder to the

kitchen and then lowered her voice so my mom wouldn't hear. "Excuse me?"

"You've got to bring him in," I said. "As long as he's out there . . ." I gestured vaguely out the French doors and past the balcony. Out to where I knew The Mole and his minions watched and waited. "Until The Mole is captured, this will never end."

Caraday quickly covered the remaining distance between us and took my hand. "We can talk about this later," she whispered. She glanced over her shoulder again. "Your mother . . ."

I nodded. Mom didn't need to know.

Agent Caraday returned to the kitchen to smooth things over with my mom. I edged closer to the door to eavesdrop. I'll give Caraday this much, she was one hell of a smooth talker. She had my mom placated inside of ten minutes, without directly lying. She assured Mom that she understood her concerns and conceded that if she had a daughter, she would probably want to be as careful. Once Mom had calmed down, they moved on to more talk about the forensic evidence they had gathered from Lévêque's body. *That* I didn't want to hear.

I wandered back to the window and stared out over the rooftops. Shadows stretched long in the late afternoon sunlight, softened by the haze of heat as if filtered through a lens.

"You hungry?"

I jumped and turned around to find Ryan standing behind me, offering a baguette sandwich. I shook my head. Despite my earlier hunger, all that talk about Lévêque's death had ruined my appetite.

"Take it." Ryan pushed it toward me. "You should always eat when you can. You never know—"

"Not you, too."

"What?"

"The mantras. That's all I ever hear from my mom. Eat when you can, sleep when you can, never jump into a conveniently waiting taxi . . ."

"She's teaching you well." He took my hand and slapped the sandwich into it. "Eat."

I sighed and took a bite to appease him. Bread and cheese never tasted better. I didn't stop until I had eaten the whole thing. "There," I said. "Are you happy?"

His mouth twisted into a smile. "Very."

"Did you know him well?"

His smile faded. "Who, Lévêque? No, I worked with him only a few times."

"So why are you here?"

"The same reason you are."

"Why is that?"

"To end this thing."

"Ah." I turned away from him and stared out the window again. I didn't know what to say to that. I wasn't sure I wanted to tell Ryan what Caraday and I had talked about. I hugged my arms. "You know what? I'm kind of tired. Can you tell my mom I'm going to lie down for a while?"

"Sure." He turned to leave the room.

"And Ryan? Thanks for the sandwich."

His smile returned. "You got it. Sweet dreams."

I curled up on the end of the sofa and I really did try to sleep. Mom should have been pleased that I was following her advice. I'd take whatever sleep I could get because once Caraday told me what she had planned, I knew it probably would be my last sleep for a long, long time.

The problem was, I was powerless to quiet the debate raging in my head. Past experience had taught me not to trust anyone and here I was considering going against my mom and putting my life in the hands of someone I didn't know. Caraday did appear to be very much involved with the investigation of Lévêque's murder, and it looked like my mom trusted her, but I'd learned long ago that appearances were not always what they seemed.

The biggest factor pushing me toward Caraday's plan was the fact that it was exactly what my mom would have done if I had been any other pawn, and not her daughter. By her own—albeit reluctant—admission, she had dangled Seth in front of The Mole's minions when they freed Seth's dad, and the operation had been a success. Apparently, this was a page right out of my mom's playbook. And now that the opportunity had come to use it against The Mole, she was allowing her emotions to cloud her judgment.

Well, I couldn't do that. I wanted my life back. And I wanted Seth to have his. The Mole had to be stopped, and if it took me squirming on the hook to catch him, that's what I would do.

I screwed my eyes shut tight and counted backward. Not from one hundred. Oh, no. My mind was much too distracted for that. I started at five hundred. I think I got down to about twenty-three before I drifted off.

When I awoke, the sky outside had turned a dusky purple. I scrubbed my hands over my eyes and tried to remember what I had dreamed. *If* I had dreamed. I wasn't sure. All I knew was that I woke with a feeling of urgency. I had to help Seth, and I had to do it immediately. I stood and padded back toward the kitchen for a drink of water. A shadowed figure stepped out from the doorway.

"It's time," Caraday said.

I nodded and drained my glass. Without a word, I followed her out the door and down the apartment building stairs. Once we had slipped outside into the balmy night air, she whispered her instructions.

"You will take the overnight train to Varese." She held out a small piece of paper. "Here is the Mulos' last known address."

"How did you get it?" I asked.

"Your mother. She doesn't know you are doing this. Are you still okay with that?"

I straightened my shoulders and nodded.

Caraday tucked the paper into my hand. "You must

memorize this address and then destroy the note, do you understand?"

Again, I nodded, my fist closing around the paper.

"The Mole will know you are coming," Caraday said softly. "He will be following you, but don't worry; he wants you and the Mulo boy together. You will reach his family unharmed. Once you are there and The Mole emerges, our operatives will take over." She handed me an envelope containing a train ticket and a small stack of Euros.

I pulled out the train ticket and stuck the envelope in the waistband of my running shorts, pulling the hem of my shirt down to cover it.

"Your train leaves for Varese in less than an hour," she whispered. "Go now."

"My mom—"

"She's sleeping. Go."

I slipped out into the shadowed streets, my heart tripping crazily. I'm sure part of that was adrenaline, but a whole lot had to do with the fact that I had no idea what I was about to get myself into.

Hurrying through the darkened street, my heart sped up even more. I wasn't sure I could find my way back to the train station in the daylight, let alone at night. I bit my lip, eyeing the shadowed doorways and alleyways, and prayed I wouldn't get lost.

For once I was glad for Mom's nagging about being aware of my surroundings because as I worked my way backward through the streets I began to recognize the boutiques and cafés Ryan and I had passed earlier that day. I also heard traffic noises just outside the quiet of the neighborhood so I knew I was headed in the right direction.

But then I heard another noise. At first I thought it was the echo of my own footsteps because the cadence matched mine exactly. I had to skip a step to avoid stepping onto a storm grate, but the footstep behind me fell without the interruption.

I thought of how I had seen Marlboro Man at the entrance to the Metro and my mouth went dry. Had he followed me? I didn't waste the time to turn around and find out, but tore down the street like my hair was on fire. I turned one corner and then another trying to shake him, but it wasn't working. I needed lights, people, attention. I slipped through a narrow alleyway and came out near a busy intersection and cut across the street. Cars swerved and honked angrily, but I didn't have time to worry about them. The Metro station lay dead ahead but not close enough; I could hear feet pounding the pavement behind me. Gaining ground.

Suddenly, a man on a bicycle swerved right in front of me, ringing his bell furiously. I reared back and jumped out of the way just in time to avoid the collision. The person behind me wasn't so lucky.

I heard the crash and the bike going down, but I wasn't about to stop to take a look. I leaped down the stairs to the Metro two at a time and pulled the ticket Caraday had given me from my pocket. When I tried to use it to release the turnstile, though, the turnstile didn't budge. I cursed under my breath. It was a long-distance train ticket and didn't work for the Metro. I shot a panicked look back at the stairs and then jumped over the machine.

A lady inside the ticket booth yelled something to me, but I couldn't stop to listen. I tore down another set of stairs to where a huge route schedule was posted on the wall. I paused long enough to find my train and platform number. My heart sank. There were ten minutes before the next train. What was I supposed to do for ten minutes? Where was I supposed to hide?

I spun around, looking for someplace—anyplace—but there was nothing, not even a bathroom to duck in to. All I saw were a handful of pay toilet booths, and I had no change.

It was well past rush hour, so only a few people milled about, waiting for the train—no crowd to get lost in. Even worse, I realized, the platform itself was a dead end. No escape routes. I was trapped.

By then I was in full panic mode. I spun around to head back to the main platform and ran smack into Ryan. He was breathing heavily and his face glistened with sweat.

He caught me as I stumbled backward. "We'll need to work on your evasion technique."

My hands curled into fists. "That was *you* chasing

after me? Why didn't you just tell me? I about had a heart attack."

"You didn't exactly hang around long enough for me to tell you anything."

"Ever heard of calling after me?"

"Would you have stopped?"

"No. Why are you following me, anyway?"

"To make sure you were safe."

I thought about me dodging cars on the boulevard and I wanted to hit him. "Go back home, Ryan. You're not going to stop me."

"Stop you from what?"

"Oh, come on. I know what you're doing."

He raised his chin, challenging. "And what is that?"

"You found out where I'm going and you came to take me back to my mom."

"Of course not," he said. "I'm coming with you."

"What? No." What was I, twelve? I didn't need him to hold my hand. "I can do this myself."

"So you know where to find your boyfriend?"

I don't know why that made me mad, but it did. Maybe because I knew it could never be true. "He's not my boyfriend," I said darkly.

Ryan started to reply, but his voice was drowned out by an incomprehensible voice coming over the loud-speakers. He cocked his head as he listened and then pointed his chin toward a long line of cars rumbling into the station. "This is our train."

"*My train*," I corrected.

"I'm coming with you."

"No, you're not."

He grabbed my shoulders and pulled me close so that his face was within inches of mine. "It's my job to protect you," he said in a low voice. "I'm coming with you."

CHAPTER
6

I stared him down. This was not the first time Ryan had told me he had been assigned to watch over me. When we were in the Cascades, he'd said the same thing. What was he, my permanent guardian? I wasn't sure if I liked the idea or resented it. In any case, it made arguing with him pointless. I had little alternative but to give in. At least for the moment. "Fine," I grumbled.

Ryan ushered me onto the train and steered me toward a couple of vacant seats. The weight of his hand on my back felt at once comforting and confining.

As soon we sat, he grabbed my hand, intertwining his fingers with mine. My eyes grew wide and I quickly tried to pull my hand away, but that only made him tighten his grip. Again I pulled and once again his fingers tightened. It was like getting caught in one of those Chinese finger traps you get at cheap arcades. Anyone looking on would think we were just two lovers holding hands, but I knew there was nothing romantic intended; Ryan had tethered me to him as surely as if he had locked handcuffs onto both our wrists. His smug smile made me want to fight. I wasn't as weak as he seemed to assume. On the other hand, any action I took would cause a scene and my mission would be over before it began. I sighed and let my hand go limp.

It wasn't until we transferred trains in Gare de Lyon that I realized Caraday had booked a private compartment for the overnight trip to Varese.

Ryan grinned like a little kid. He plopped down on one bench seat and stretched out his legs, resting his feet on the opposite bench. "Perfect." He tucked his hands behind his head. "Maybe we can catch a few Z's on the way."

That left me with no other option than to take the seat next to Ryan.

Suddenly, I didn't know what to do with myself. I folded and unfolded my hands in my lap, crossed and uncrossed my legs. Finally, I hugged my arms and stared out the window—anything to avoid looking him in the face. Several hours of awkwardness alone in a dark, enclosed space with Ryan was not exactly what I had in mind when I signed up for the assignment. I would have preferred to make the ride alone.

He must have misinterpreted my unease because he reached across the empty space between us and placed his hand on my knee. "You okay with this?"

I stared at his hand, a wave of heat spreading across my face. "What do you mean?"

"What they're having you do. You can still back out, you know."

"Oh." I dragged my eyes away from his hand on my knee and searched his face. Was he saying I was a coward? "I won't back out."

"I didn't think you would."

"You understand why I have to do this, then."

He cocked his head and gave me a solemn once-over. "Yeah. 'Cause you're your mother's daughter."

I frowned, hugging my arms even tighter.

"What? You don't think so?"

I shrugged. "I know I'm her daughter."

"But?"

"But I'm not sure what that means."

"It means that this is in your blood."

"This what? What are you talking about?"

Ryan spread his hands. "This. The life. You can't leave well enough alone. You have to know what makes things tick . . . and then you have to do something about it. Just like your mom."

I wanted to deny what he was saying was true, but it had been my inability to leave well enough alone that got me mixed up with the Mulos in the first place, and I'm sure Ryan knew that. He probably had a file on me somewhere if he was supposed to be my bodyguard or whatever. He would know that when the Mulos came to our island, I couldn't rest until I discovered who they really were and what they were up to. And by the time I found that out, I was neck deep in intrigue and it was impossible to walk away.

"Is it in *your* blood?" I asked.

He grinned, his teeth flashing white in the darkness. "Hell, yeah."

I latched on to his enthusiasm, hoping to steer the conversation away from me. "Runs in your family?"

His smile faltered. "Yes," he said after a moment, "yes, it does."

I realized that I must have struck a nerve, but I didn't know what I should do about it—stay clear or keep pressing. I didn't have to decide, though, because he took the initiative. "It's not always black and white," he said. "Sometimes you can pursue one dream only at the expense of another."

"I'm not sure I—"

"Your mom is fiercely proud of you, Aphra. She must have really trusted that you were ready to find your way, or she wouldn't have let the job's call take over."

I blinked. How had he done that? He switched from his nerve to mine so smoothly I never saw it coming. Well, I wasn't going to play into his hands. I steered back into safe territory.

"Why did you follow me to Paris?" I asked.

He didn't hesitate. "To keep an eye on you."

"So you didn't trust my mom to keep me safe?"

"Listen, Aphra." His voice grew serious. "When that ring of Mulo's revealed the list of The Mole's associates, we were able to capture most of them. But a handful, including The Mole, just went further underground.

Until we can account for every name on that list, you are my responsibility."

That was sobering enough to keep me quiet for a moment, but then I had to ask, "So you don't think what I'm doing, going to Varese and all, is dangerous?"

"On the contrary. I think it's very dangerous. That's why I'm riding along."

"Oh." I let that sink in for a moment, but it didn't compute. "So you're supposed to be protecting me, but you don't mind if I do something that might get me hurt."

"Oh, I mind," Ryan said. "But I wasn't joking when I told you I thought you'd be an asset to the Agency. You need to have the experience of an op to see what it's all about." He grinned again. "Then you'll be hooked."

I gave him half a nod. What he didn't understand was a lot. He really thought it was going to help me to think that my mom was willing to leave me and my dad because being an agent was just too thrilling to give up? Maybe that was his incentive for sticking with it, but I would never believe it was hers. I couldn't.

I turned from him and closed my eyes. His words chanted in my head with the rhythm of the wheels on the tracks: *You'll be hooked, you'll be hooked, you'll be hooked.* No, he didn't understand me at all.

I woke sometime after midnight. The sway of the train had changed; we were slowing down. With a jolt

I realized I was leaning against Ryan's shoulder and I quickly sat up. "Are we there?"

"No. We've only just crossed the border."

"Maybe they need to check our passports."

"They don't do that within the EU. Once you're in, you can travel anywhere." He checked his watch and peered out the window. "We shouldn't be stopping. Sit still. I'm going to check and see what has happened."

Ryan ducked out into the aisle and I rushed to the doorway to watch him go. At the end of the car, a man in a conductor uniform stood talking on a two-way radio and gesturing wildly with his free hand. Ryan didn't even talk to the guy; he just stood there and listened, and then he came back to report to me. He ushered me back inside the compartment.

"You're not going to believe this; the train ahead of us hit a cow and several cars derailed."

"No way. A cow?"

"That's what the man said. Line's closed from here to Omegna until they can clear it off."

"How long will that take?"

"Emergency crews have been summoned, he says, but no telling how long it will be until they arrive."

"So what do we do?" I tried to sound calm, but inside the panic was rising again. The whole operation could be thrown off if I wasn't on my mark by morning. Caraday had said that The Mole hadn't found the Mulos *yet*, but I didn't doubt that he would, and that he would hurt Seth's family if I wasn't there as the sacrificial lamb.

"First thing we do is clear the train. They're ordering everyone off."

There was nothing to be done but to join the rest of the grumbling passengers in our car filing down the narrow aisle and out the door. A uniformed train worker stood on the platform, directing people into the station. If his haggard face and drooping posture were any indication, he was as tired as we were and just as irritated by the inconvenience.

Apparently, the station itself was not prepared to accommodate travelers in the middle of the night. The lights were on, but nothing was open—not the ticket booths or the stationmaster's office or any of the small shops that lined the perimeter. The only place to go was into a small lobby area, where there weren't nearly enough chairs for everyone to sit.

I wasn't worried about the seating arrangements, though. I kept glancing at the huge round clock on the far wall, calculating and recalculating how much time we had left before showtime. Impatience buzzed through me. I paced. The room was too small, too crowded. I was suffocating. And I had to get to Varese.

Ryan wandered over to the ticket counter and grabbed a train schedule printout. He brought it over to me and we scanned it together, looking for an alternate route or some other alternative that would get us to Varese on time.

And then I smelled it. The strange sour stench I noticed every time I caught the Marlboro Man following me. My heart lodged in my chest like a chunk of ice. I turned slowly, scanning the crowd. I couldn't see him, but I knew he was there.

I grabbed Ryan's hand. "We need to get out of here," I hissed. "Now."

He leaned close, a sleepy smile on his lips, but I saw the way his eyes became sharp, alert. "What is it?" he whispered.

I didn't have time for explanations. "We need to *go*," I insisted.

To his credit, Ryan didn't press me again, but quickly steered me toward the tall wooden doors at the front of the station. I don't know what made me turn my head. Premonition, maybe? All I know is that just as I reached for the metal bar handle of the door, I felt an uncomfortable tingle at the back of my neck and glanced behind me.

The room went black—or so it seemed. All I could see for that awful moment was the angry face of the Marlboro Man as he fixed his cold eyes on me. Ryan must have noticed him, too, because he tightened his grip on my hand and yanked me with him as he pushed through the door and out into the night. It didn't occur to me at the time to wonder if Ryan recognized the man or why he would have been alarmed to see him.

Ryan slowed for a heartbeat as he turned his head left

and then right, assessing the escape routes, I figured, since he pulled me to the right and down a short flight of stone steps and into the shadows. Behind us, I heard the door bang open again. I didn't have to look back to know it would be Marlboro Man, but looking was the immediate reaction to the banging door. Sure enough, it was him. And he was carrying a gun. Suddenly, my back felt like an open target. It spurred me to run even faster, to push my stride longer to keep up with Ryan so I wouldn't slow him down.

Ahead to one side lay a huge open field, backed by a deep stand of trees. On the other side, a two-lane road wound down a hill, presumably into the town, lit at regular intervals by the soft glow of streetlights and fading away into the gathering mist. Either route would leave us vulnerable, exposed, but at least the field was cloaked in darkness, and if we made it across the field alive, we might be able to hide in the trees. I pulled on Ryan's hand this time, veering into the field. He adjusted his course without question. I wondered if it was because he trusted my instincts or because he had the same idea himself.

We bounded through the field, high-stepping over the rows of some kind of vining crop. Weak moonlight skittered ahead of us, along straight, narrow rows of stubby vegetation that caught on our feet and threatened to trip us if we weren't careful where we stepped. By the time we were halfway across the field, my muscles felt like burning rubber, and my chest was a hot, tight vise, forbidding me to catch my breath.

I could hear heavy footsteps crashing through the field behind us. We were close, so close to the cover of the trees, but close wasn't going to cut it. I wondered who Marlboro would try to take down first. Probably Ryan. I would be easier to catch. But the guy never fired a shot. Maybe he preferred to do his work at close range.

When we reached the safety of the tree trunks, I could have cheered, but I knew I had to save my breath. The chase was not nearly over. Ryan took the lead again, dodging around trees, trailing me behind him like a child's toy. Moonlight filtered through the leaves above us, casting Rorschach shadows on the ground, and camouflaging the terrain so that we couldn't tell if we were about to trip on a rock or step into a hole. I twisted my ankle more than once and nearly fell on my face, but Ryan held me up. Ryan kept me going.

The moonlight faded as we pushed deeper into the woods, and at first I thought it was because the trees were so much thicker, but as it grew darker and darker, I glanced up to see that heavy clouds had swept across the sky, blotting out the moon and whatever light it might have offered. Which was good because it meant we would be hidden in the darkness, but not so great because it was getting to the point that we could barely see three feet in front of us.

From behind—I couldn't tell how close—came a

sharp crack as if someone had stepped on a very large twig. I tugged on Ryan's hand to signal him to stop. We pressed our backs up against a tree trunk and waited. I wanted to gulp in great rasps of air, but I forced myself to breathe silently, easy in, easy out, until I thought I would choke. There wasn't much I could do about my thundering heartbeat, though. I closed my eyes, wincing with every *ba-bump*, quite sure that Marlboro Man would have had to be deaf not to hear it.

I heard him pass by. I didn't dare turn my head to visually verify it was him, but I didn't really have to. I could smell—the burnt-tar stench, now mixed with pungent BO. That was enough for me.

Ryan shifted so that his body was shielding mine against the tree and he stood there, pressed up against me, until Marlboro Man was long gone and his odor faded away. It made me feel, if not exactly safe, at least protected. Grudgingly, I had to admit that I was actually glad that Ryan had insisted on coming along. I would have preferred it to be Seth pressing me up against the tree, but that was a thought for another time. Our only concern at the moment was getting out of the woods undetected and finding our way to Varese.

Suddenly, Ryan was gone from me. He sprang into the darkness and I heard scuffling to my left. Someone grunted. It didn't sound like Ryan. And then I heard a heavy thud and the ground vibrated beneath my feet.

Ryan returned, out of breath. "Let's go. Quickly." He took my hand again.

"Is he . . . ?"

"He's out, for the moment."

"What about his gun?"

Ryan grinned as he held the weapon up so it could catch the faint moonlight. "No worries," he said, and tucked the gun into the back of his waistband underneath his shirt. He led the way through the trees double-time. I had to practically run to keep up with him, but I wasn't going to argue. I kept thinking that Marlboro Man could wake up at any moment and when he did, he'd be plenty angry. I didn't want to be anywhere in the vicinity when that happened.

Eventually, the trees thinned and spilled out of the woods near a paved road. Not the same road we had seen that led into town, I guessed, since this one was flat and straight, whereas the other had curved away from the station.

"What now?" I whispered.

"We keep moving."

"How close are we to Varese? Can we take a taxi?"

He snorted. "We're not that close."

"Can we take one to the next station? Beyond the cow on the tracks?"

He nodded. "That's the idea. We just need to figure out how to get there."

"There was a taxi stand back at the station. . . ."

"No good," he said. "Our friend back there could be waiting for us."

"The city center, then. It can't be far from the station, can it? Do you think this road connects with the other one?"

Ryan hitched his hands on his hips and peered through the darkness. "Only one way to find out."

We followed the road, walking on the pavement because it was easier than navigating the uneven ground. A breeze had picked up and I, in just the tank and shorts, started to shiver. Not horribly, but enough that Ryan noticed.

"Here. Take this," Ryan said. He peeled off his jacket and draped it over my shoulders. I tried to give it back—I was beginning to feel just a little too much like a damsel in distress—but he glowered at me. "Put it on."

I figured it probably wasn't worth the argument, so I slipped my arms into the sleeves. Just then, two beams of light swept toward us down the road.

Ryan grabbed me and pulled me off to the side. "Stay low," he warned. "We don't know who it might be."

I ducked low as he was doing until the lights drew nearer and a delivery truck came into focus. "A ride!" I jumped up and waved my arms madly to flag it down. The truck passed slowly, but then rolled to a stop just a few yards ahead of us, the red taillights glowing like hot coals. I ran toward them.

"Wait!" Ryan yelled after me. "Be careful!"

But I had already reached the cab. The trucker powered down his window and asked if we needed a lift. *"Volete un passaggio?"*

"Sì, fantastico. Grazie!" I said. Yes, please!

Ryan was at my side before I could reach the door handle. He grabbed my arm. "What do you think you're doing?"

I pulled away from him. "I'm going to Varese. Are you coming?"

The driver leaned toward the passenger seat and said in English, "I don't go to Varese. But I can take you as far as Cassano Magnago, *sì?"*

I didn't know where Cassano Magnago was, but it must have been on the way to Varese if the driver said he could take us "as far as." And it would be farther away from Marlboro Man than we were at the moment. *"Sì,"* I said, and climbed up to the cab. *"Grazie."*

Ryan made an exasperated growling sound, but he climbed up behind me just the same.

The cab of the truck had obviously not been designed for three passengers and the fit was tight. Still, our driver appeared to be very pleased to have company for the long, dark drive ahead. He shoved a couple of notebooks and paper bags that had been sitting next to him underneath the seat and brushed the bench free of any crumbs there might have been—though it's not likely he could have seen them in the dark.

"I am Salvatore," he said, touching a meaty hand to his chest.

"*Buona sera*, Salvatore," I replied. "I'm Donna and this is John. Thank you so much for offering us a ride."

"Ah, Donna!" He grinned broadly, gold tooth catching the light from the dash. "An Italian name, yes?"

I nodded slowly, settling onto the seat. "Uh . . . yes. Of course. I am named for my grandmother who lives in Varese."

"Wonderful, wonderful," Salvatore exclaimed. "You are American?"

"Canadian," I said, giving him a winning smile.

Ryan slammed the door shut behind himself, and Salvatore released the emergency brake. "I have been to Canada once." As tight as we were in the cab, I was practically straddling the gearshift, but it didn't seem to bother Salvatore. He ground the gears into first. "Many years ago. I see the Niagara Falls."

Ryan fell easily into our fictional personas. "My cousin lives near Niagara Falls," he said. "Plays for the Bills."

"*American* football?" Salvatore sounded genuinely mortified.

"He's big," Ryan said, "but he doesn't have the speed to play regular football."

"*Sì, certo, certo*," Salvatore mused. "One must have speed for the football."

"I hope to see Inter Milan play while we are here," Ryan said.

That was all Salvatore needed to hear. He launched into a lengthy description of the soccer team's strengths and weaknesses. I had no idea what he was talking about, but Ryan seemed to be getting into it.

Between the drone of their voices, the darkness outside, and the hum of the tires on the road, I began to feel drowsy. I fought it; even though I didn't know when I might sleep next, we were in a stranger's truck and I knew I should stay alert. But then I figured that Ryan was alert enough for the both of us and I let my eyelids shut longer and longer each time I blinked. I kept drifting in and out of their conversation. By the time I heard the gears shift down as the truck slowed, I was nearly catatonic.

Salvatore pulled over to the side of the road. "Only five kilometers that way you will find the Cassano Magnago station," he said as we climbed down from the cab.

"Thank you very much. *Grazie!*"

We stood and waved as he pulled back onto the main road. My brain was so tired I couldn't even think straight.

"Five kilometers . . ." I asked sleepily. "That's how far again?"

"Just over three miles," Ryan said.

"Then we better get walking."

The first thing I noticed as we crunched along the lonely road was that the dark clouds overhead seemed to be lower than they had been before. The second thing I noticed was that on this road, unlike the larger road we had just left, no streetlights lit the way. We literally had to stumble along through the dark.

And then it began to rain. The drops started out small and tentative as if they were scoping out the countryside before planning an assault with the bigger artillery. Sure enough, they grew bolder. Like the rain at the cemetery, big, fat drops soaked through our clothes and splashed up from the ground at our feet.

Ryan pointed to what looked to be a farming shed about one city block down the road. "Come on!"

I didn't need any more encouragement than that. He grabbed my hand and we ran through the rain to the shed, only to find it closed up tight, with a padlock hanging from the door.

"Hold on." Ryan pulled out the gun.

"Wait! Don't *shoot* it." I tried to grab his arm, but he shook me off.

"We'll leave some money for repairs," he said, and pointed the gun at the door. He fired and the lock fell open. Rolling the door back, he shooed me inside.

I couldn't really see much of the place, but I could smell it. Fresh dirt, old hay, and very possibly natural fertilizer gave the place a pungent, very farm-y odor. Once my eyes adjusted, I could see a tractor with a miniature flatbed attached to it sitting in the middle of the shed. Stacks of hay bales lined one wall and an array of farm implements hung on the other.

I had to admit that I was glad Ryan had destroyed the lock so that we could duck inside. Not more than a minute after we did, the sky ripped open and water poured down in solid sheets. With the rain, the temperature dropped even more and sucked away what little heat I had left in my body. I shivered so hard my teeth chattered and my back ached.

Ryan stood in the doorway, his tall figure silhouetted black against the lesser black of the storm. "Why don't you lie down and get some rest?" He said. "I'll keep watch."

Again, my sense of feminism bristled. I could stand watch just as well as he could. But I was tired. So very, very tired. And then there was my mom's voice echoing in my head. *Sleep when you can. Sleep when you can.*

I let my eyes stray to the hay bales and considered that it wouldn't hurt to close my eyes, just for a moment. Then I would trade places with Ryan and let him sleep. It seemed like an equitable arrangement to my tired mind. I drew Ryan's jacket around me and curled up on the hay and before I knew it, I was out.

CHAPTER
7

I saw Seth in my dreams. I was sitting on the shore, watching the waves curl inland when he emerged from the sea like Poseidon's warrior, sun glistening across his chest and on his wet, slicked-back hair. He strolled toward me purposefully. Water dripped from the hem of his board shorts, pooling at his feet, bringing the ocean with him.

He dropped to the sand beside me and pulled me into his arms. I snuggled up to him, curving my arm around his neck to draw him closer. He brushed the hair from my face and whispered my name.

"Aphra."

But the voice wasn't his.

All too soon I remembered where I was. Where *we* were. *Ryan, not Seth*, I thought, disappointed.

Ryan's fingers whispered across my cheek as he brushed back a stray strand of hair. "Aphra, are you awake?"

I'm not sure why I didn't answer him. I think it was something in his voice, like he was checking not to see if I was awake, but to make sure that I was asleep. I lay deathly still and waited to see why. Silence roared in my ears. And then Ryan's footsteps creaked across the floor of the shed, moving away from me. The rollers softly protested when he opened the door. I heard the gravel crunch beneath his feet as he stepped outside.

I sat up, feeling like a heavy stone had just been dropped square in the middle of my chest. From outside the shed I heard the low register of Ryan's voice. He was talking to someone. Talking in a furtive, don't-let-the-girl-hear kind of way.

I leaned forward, straining to make out the words. What was he saying? Who was he talking to? I stared at the pale shaft of moonlight spilling across the floor from where the door had not completely shut. *The rain must have moved on*, I thought absently.

And then I caught the urgent tone of Ryan's voice. I didn't like the way it sounded. Slowly, carefully, I scooted to the edge of the hay bales and pushed myself to my feet. I tiptoed across the wooden floor and hovered just inside the door.

". . . lucky to even find a signal. Yeah. We're near Cassano Magnago, probably another hour or so to Varese." He listened. "What? Are you ser— No, I know what you're saying. Right. Yeah, she's sleeping. . . . No, I'm not going to tell her. She'll come along; she trusts me. . . . Right. We'll see you in Milan."

His phone snapped shut and I backed away from the crack in the door. I leaped for the bales just as I heard the door squeak open. Squeezing my eyes shut, I tried to pretend I was sleeping, but what I really wanted to do was to scream. I couldn't believe that just hours before, I had felt safe and secure with Ryan, when all along he'd been lying to me. What wasn't he going to tell me? That we were diverting to Milan? The secretive tone of his voice played over in my head and I could have slugged him. *She trusts me. . . .* Yeah, right. Not anymore.

Ryan's footsteps drew nearer. He sat down beside me. "Aphra," he called softly.

It was all I could do not to rear up and slap him in the face. Instead I rolled over and squinted up at him. "Hnnnh?"

"It's stopped raining."

I sat up, smoothing back my hair. "What time is it?"

"Six o'clock."

"*Six?*" I hadn't realized I had slept that long. I bolted off the bale of hay. "What time is the train?"

"Relax. We're not far from the station. We still have about a half hour."

Sure. If we wanted to catch the train to Milan. I pulled off Ryan's jacket and shoved it at him. "Here. Thanks for letting me use it."

He blinked at me. "Uh, okay. You sure you don't need it anymore?"

I headed for the door. "I'm positive."

He was right; the station wasn't far at all. Just down the road, past the hay fields and over a gentle rise. In the early morning light and with the mist left from the rain, the farmland we were hiking through looked like a pastoral painting. But I was much too angry to enjoy the scenery. He lied to me. He *was lying* to me. My mom was right; you can't trust anyone.

We'd only been walking for maybe fifteen minutes before I could see the tracks curve ahead and not long after that, the hipped roof of the station.

I did a lot of thinking in those fifteen minutes, and although I ended up with more questions than answers, one thing I knew for sure was that there was no way I was going to Milan. Not with the remaining threat against Seth and his family. I could only assume Ryan had been talking to the Agency, and no matter what they said, I wasn't going to abandon the Mulos.

How I was going to escape from Ryan was another matter. He wasn't going to let me just walk away. I thought of how he'd chased me the night before and I knew I wasn't going to outrun him, either. He'd said I needed to work on my evasion technique. Fine. That's exactly what I'd do.

As Ryan bought our tickets, I studied the schedule on the wall. It was six twenty-two. The train to Milan headed south from track four in six minutes. The train we *should* be taking curved north to Porto Ceresio, stopping in Varese. It left in twelve minutes. What made him think I would be stupid enough not to know the difference? Because I trusted him? Wrong.

I pretended not to notice the destination clearly posted next to the door and allowed him to lead me onto the deception train.

We found two empty seats together and Ryan stepped aside so I could take the one by the window. Or, more likely, so that he could box me in. I closed my eyes, resting my head against the back of the seat.

"You still tired?" Ryan asked.

"*Sì.*" I answered, without looking at him. Tired of being lied to.

Soon, the voice on the train's intercom announced our imminent departure. I stood. "Excuse me," I said.

Ryan glanced up, startled. "Where are you going?"

I gave him a pained look. "I need to . . . you know." I jerked my head toward the restrooms at the end of the car.

"Oh."

I climbed over him and hurried down the aisle, feeling his eyes on my back the entire time. I glanced at my watch. The train should leave in less than a minute. I reached the doors to the bathroom. Thirty seconds. Paused. Twenty seconds. I kept walking to the vestibule. Ten seconds. Ryan bolted out of his chair and started charging down the aisle toward me. The chime sounded overhead. Five seconds. I slipped out the doors just before they closed.

Standing on the platform, I watched as the train sighed and shuddered forward. Inside, Ryan slammed his fist against the window, yelling something I couldn't understand.

I cupped my hand to my ear and mouthed, "I can't hear you." The car passed and Ryan was gone.

According to what the schedule had said, I had six minutes before the train for Varese departed. I scurried into the station and bought a non-reserved ticket to Varese and then rushed back to track number one where the train idled, its engine harnessed and humming. Passing up the line of reserved-seating cars, I found one with a non-reserved sign toward the rear of the train and climbed on board.

There were only five other people scattered throughout the car. Three of them were sleeping—one snoring loudly—one man was reading the newspaper, and a guy with a huge backpack in the seat next to him was holding his cell phone in both hands, thumbs moving at lightning speed. None of them looked up.

I chose a seat two rows back from the snorer—far enough away that I had a little space, but close enough that I wouldn't stand out as the lone person if anyone glanced into the car.

It wasn't until the train had left the station that I started having second thoughts about ditching Ryan. Once the adrenaline wore off, I had to admit that I didn't actually know what I was going to do once I reached Varese. Besides find Seth, I mean. But being bait didn't seem like such a smart idea if there were no longer a trap. If the Agency had withdrawn its support—which I had to assume was true since Ryan was supposed to divert me to Milan—then we would be on our own.

What I didn't understand was *why* they would have diverted. When Caraday had spoken to me, she'd sounded so intent on carrying out the mission. Like it was as personal to her as it was to me. I couldn't imagine her changing her mind in less than six hours. Unless . . . I flopped back against my seat and groaned. My mom. She probably pitched a fit when she found out where I had gone. I could just see her demanding that they yank me from the job. I didn't know what kind of pull she had with the Agency, but given her top secret status, it was probably substantial.

I had one of those heart-dragging, gut-sinking feelings you get when you're waiting for the next shoe to drop. I was going to be in major trouble when she caught up with me. But how could that be worse than not doing anything and knowing that I would never have a normal life? Even if the Agency happened to warn the Mulos this time, unless they caught The Mole, the cycle would just continue again and again and again. Couldn't they see that by now?

All they had to do was look at how he had chased the Mulos over the years. Everywhere they had run, the Mole had come after them. He found them in California and Michigan, he found them on our island, he found them when they split up and now he'd found them in Italy.

What would stop him from finding them again? Or finding my mom and me?

Plus there was the way he had managed to infiltrate their own Agency. Weren't they the least bit worried about that? He had been able to embed a spy in my mom's operation in Seattle and he'd known exactly where we were in Paris. There was no reason to believe he would quit stalking any of us . . . unless he was caught.

Caraday was right; to catch The Mole, the Agency had to flush him out. Why weren't they doing that?

I probably would have dwelled on that particular point a bit longer, but my attention was drawn to the conductor in his dark blue suit, making his way through the car, punching tickets with a distinct *kachink, kachink*. I fidgeted and waited until he reached my seat and asked for my ticket.

"Il biglietto, per favore, signorina."

I handed it to him and he started to punch it, but then he stopped. He looked at me, then at my ticket, then at me again.

"You are English?" he said with a heavy accent.

My stomach dropped. Had Ryan alerted the train already? How was that possible? They were going to stop me. They were going to make me get off. They—

"Mi dispiace," the conductor said. "I am sorry, but this ticket goes to Varese."

"Yes," I said, not comprehending. "That's where I'm going."

"But this train come *from* Varese. We stop next in Vergiate."

"No." I felt like I'd just been dropped into a bad dream. Air rushed in my ears. I could barely feel my hand clutching the ticket. "But the sign said—"

"Mi dispiace," he repeated. "But no worry. There will be a train in Vergiate to take you to Varese."

I thanked him and slouched down in my seat, fighting back tears of frustration. How could I have done something so idiotic? Now there was no way I'd make it to Varese by eight A.M. as The Mole demanded. I stared out the window at the scenery—like a movie set rolling past—my stomach cranking tighter and tighter with every turn of the wheel until I thought I was going to be sick.

When we stopped in Vergiate, I slogged off the train and then watched in miserable frustration as it screeched and shuddered and rolled away from the station. The schedule board showed two trains headed to Varese— one in ten minutes and one in an hour.

I ran inside and bought a ticket from the machine to cover the ride from Vergiate to Cassano Magnago. From there, I could use my original ticket to get to Varese. I felt supremely stupid that I had to get myself back to where I had started from before I could move forward. By now it was already after seven. Because of my stupid mistake, I would never reach Varese on time. I don't know what The Mole planned to do if Seth and I weren't "delivered" by his eight A.M. deadline, but based on his track record, I didn't want to find out. Of course, I didn't exactly want to find out what he would do if he got a hold of us, either.

I paced, checking my watch every two minutes, and tried to formulate some kind of plan of action for when I caught up with the Mulos at the address Caraday had given me. The whole idea was to ensnare The Mole. Maybe if we led them on a chase to Milan . . . And then it hit me. Milan. Ryan would never dare show up there without me. He knew me. As soon as I stepped off that train, he had to know what I was planning to do. The first chance he got, I had no doubt Ryan would sound the alarm and come after me. By going on to Varese, I was essentially forcing their hand. Regardless of what my mom wanted, we would carry on with the operation as planned. At least that's what I hoped would happen.

There was one small hitch in my imagined scenario: Ryan could not have known that I would have gotten on a train headed in the opposite direction. They would have no idea where I was or when I was arriving in Varese. Or if I *was* arriving in Varese. My heart sank. I might have to go it alone after all.

Finally, an announcement echoed through the passenger concourse. I couldn't quite hear all the words, but I think it was saying that my train had just arrived. I rushed out to the platform. The train was there, but so were a whole lot of people, lined up at each car, waiting to board. Rush hour. I joined the queue at one of the back cars—I had bought an unreserved seat again, in case a name or identification was required to make a reservation. Suddenly, I wished that I had taken the chance and selected a seat.

By the time I entered the car, it was almost completely full. Ours was not the first stop on the line, and the train must have already been crowded. I scanned the seats as I wandered through the car, but I wasn't able to find one to myself. Worse, all the aisle seats had been taken so I'd be boxed in, no matter where I sat.

I ended up choosing a seat near the rear of the car so that if I had to leave in a hurry, at least I'd be near an exit. On the downside, my seatmate, a burly guy with oiled hair and several heavy gold chains around his neck, seemed to be watching me, waiting for me to meet his gaze. I turned as far from him as I could without being blatantly rude. No need to give him a reason to remember me. One of the advantages of the window seat, I supposed, was that I could pretend to be engrossed in the scenery—even if we were just sitting at the station.

As it was, sitting at the station gave me too much time to think. And my thoughts kept slipping back to Ryan, no matter how I tried to divert them. Two opposing images flashed through my head. The first was Ryan, shielding me by the tree, handing me his jacket, brushing the hair from my face when he thought I was asleep. But then there was the other image—Ryan outside the shed, pressing the cell phone to his ear, telling the Agency how he was going to trick me into going to Milan. I didn't know how both images could be the same person.

Meanwhile, more than an hour away, Seth and his parents were in danger and if the stupid train didn't start moving soon, I was going to be too late to do anything about it.

Finally, we dragged slowly and sluggishly forward before picking up speed and leaving the station behind. Outside, the early-morning sun had painted the sky a salmon pink and gilded the clouds left over from the night's rain. The train wound its way around a blue-gray lake, the waves blushing in reflection of the sky. If the circumstances had been different, I might have appreciated the beauty of it. As it was, the lake stood in the way of Seth, and all I wanted was to put it behind me.

CHAPTER
8

The train sighed into Varese just after eight in the morning. A full hour later than I planned to have met the Mulos. In the vestibule, I danced from foot to foot and waited for the doors to release. The second they hissed open, I jumped forward like a sprinter out of the gate.

I ran, weaving through commuters and tourists, students and working men. The acoustics of the tile floors and the granite walls of the passenger concourse magnified and jumbled their voices until it sounded like a loud, echoing henhouse.

At each turn, I half expected Ryan to step out and demand to know what I was doing. When I didn't see him, I was at once relieved and disappointed. But I didn't have time to worry about him. I had to get to the Mulos' apartment.

In the front of the station, a group of cabbies clustered together, smoking and laughing. One of them—a stout man in a leather vest and matching ivy-style cap, glanced over at me as I rushed outside. He threw his cigarette down and ground it out with the toe of his boot.

"Taxi, signorina?" he asked.

"Sì, grazie!" To my ears, my voice came out high-pitched and shrill. I took a deep breath before giving him the address. *"Ho fretta,"* I added. I'm in a hurry.

He hurried to open the door of his boxy white car and bustled me into the back. I had barely gotten both legs inside when he slammed the door behind me.

Jumping into the driver's seat, he set the meter running, then shot away from the curb so fast that the force of it threw me backward. I sprawled across the seat, gripping the door handle as we whipped through the winding streets. All I saw of the city was a blur of white buildings with terra-cotta roofs, deep green vegetation, bright flowers in window boxes, and laundry waving on the lines overhead.

Finally, the taxi screeched to a stop and the driver announced we had arrived. I peered out the window at a three-story apartment building, square and squat with a shallow, hipped roof.

"Grazie," I said shakily. I handed him a twenty-euro bill for a six-fifty fare, but I wasn't about to hang around for the change. I jumped from the cab and ran for the entrance.

Unfortunately, the entry to this building, like the apartment back in Paris, was controlled by a panel of buttons, each labeled with a surname, presumably of the person or family who lived in the apartment. No numbers. How was anyone supposed to find a specific apartment that way? I ran my finger down the list of names. Not that I had imagined I would see the name Mulo, but

I had hoped for something overly common like Smith, or, since we were in Italy, Rossi. No such luck.

The only thing I could think of to do was to buzz each apartment in turn until I hit the right one. With luck, there wouldn't be anything like a three-tries-you're-out feature in the control box.

I buzzed the first one. No response, so I buzzed the next button down. The intercom at the base of the box crackled.

A woman's voice demanded to know who was there.

"Elena?" I asked.

She snapped that I had the wrong house.

I hit button number three. Again, no response. Just as I was about to buzz the next one down, a lanky guy in too-tight spandex shorts pushed out the door, shouldering a sleek racing bicycle. *"Permesso,"* he said. Excuse me.

"Non importa," I assured him, and stepped aside, holding the door for him. And then I let myself into the building.

As soon as he left, I tore up the stairs to the second floor and searched the numbers on the doors until I came to 2C. When I saw it, my heart twisted in my chest. The door to the apartment stood partially open.

A cold sense of foreboding slithered down my back and I flattened myself against the wall. I'm not sure how long I stood there, holding my breath, listening for sounds from inside the apartment, but it felt like a long,

long time. Only when I didn't hear anything did I dare to slide cautiously toward the door.

With the toe of my shoe, I pushed the door open just a little bit farther and peeked inside. I didn't see any movement.

"Hello?" I called softly.

No answer. I pushed the door open even wider and took a tentative step inside. And then I knew. The Mulos had already gone. It looked like they left in a hurry, too. In the small kitchenette to my right, dishes still sat in the sink. Some of the drawers were pulled partially open. To my left, a magazine lay open on a glass-topped coffee table in front of a sleek leather couch, a half-empty glass of water on a coaster beside it.

Tears blurred my vision and I wiped them away with the back of my hand. I was too late. The knowledge left me dead and hollow inside. I turned to leave the apartment when I caught a flash of silver on the floor next to the couch. I bent to pick it up. A knot tightened in my throat as it dangled from my fingers. I recognized it at once; it was the chain I had worn to hold Seth's ring. The clasp had broken. I wondered when that had happened. How it had happened.

"Ferma!" A deep voice behind me ordered. Halt.

I jumped and spun around. A tall man in a dark wool suit and narrow tie stood in the doorway, his black eyes fixed on me as if he'd just found a cockroach skittering along the floor. *"Cosa sta facendo?"* he demanded. What are you doing?

My mind raced. What could I say? Definitely not that I knew the people who had lived in the apartment. Then he might ask me who they were. *"Mi scusi,"* I apologized. *"Ho visto la porta aperta. . . ."* The door was open. . . .

He strode forward so that he hovered over me, his expression, if possible, soured even more than before. "You are American?"

I nodded, mouth too dry to speak.

He fished a leather wallet decorated with a brass shield from his pocket and waved it at me. "I am police. You cannot be here."

"I'm sorry. I'll leave." I tried to move past him, but he blocked my way.

"No. You are looting. For this, I must arrest you."

My eyes grew wide as I followed his pointed glare to the chain I held in my hand. "Oh, no! I wasn't stealing this. It's—"

"I advise you to say nothing further. You may call your consulate from the station. They will arrange the lawyer."

I shook my head. That was one thing I couldn't do. Not unless I wanted the consulate to find out that the person on my passport didn't exist. "Look, I seriously was not loo—"

He pulled a pair of handcuffs from his pocket. "Turn around."

I shrank back. No. This was all wrong. "Could I please see that badge again?"

"Turn around. Now." He pushed back his suit coat enough that I could see a pistol in the holster at his belt.

I stared at the gun. I wasn't exactly familiar with the Italian police procedure, but the arrest scenario didn't feel right. Something was definitely off. I didn't believe for a moment that he was a real policeman. But that only made things worse for me. It meant that he wouldn't have to play by the rules. I turned slowly, keeping my hands where he could see them. He already looked pretty agitated and I didn't want to give him any reason to reach for that gun. He yanked first one hand and then the other behind my back and snapped the cold, metal cuffs onto my wrists, squeezing them so that they clicked small enough to pinch. I bit my lips to keep from crying out. But when he yanked the chain from my hand, I couldn't help it.

"Save your breath, *signorina*," he said, and grabbed my arm to spin me around. "We go now."

I could hear doors open and caught a few curious neighbors gawking from their *appartamenti* as he marched me down the stairs and through the tiled entry. I kept my head down as we went, not out of shame, but to hide my face so that the black-eyed "policeman" wouldn't see how my eyes darted from door to door, searching for a familiar face, for an escape route, for anything that would get me out of the mess I had gotten myself into.

He marched me out to the street where a sleek silver car waited at the curb, its domed blue light spinning in flashing circles from the dashboard. More neighbors huddled in a curious cluster on the sidewalk, watching and whispering at a safe distance.

The fake policeman yelled at them to go back to their business. *"Tornate ai vostri affari!"* He opened the door of the car and then pushed me forward, grabbing my skull like a bowling ball so that I wouldn't smack my head on the top of the door frame—as if I didn't have the intelligence to duck. His fingers dug into my scalp and I flinched, which must have made him think I was trying to break away from him because he pushed me even harder and the force of it made me stumble. I fell forward so that only the top part of my body made it onto the seat, my legs sprawled out behind me.

"Get up," Black Eyes ordered. But since my hands were cuffed behind my back, it's not like I could push myself up. I struggled to find my balance, let alone the momentum to rise to my feet. Impatient with my slow response, he grabbed one of my arms and yanked it back even harder. New pain ripped through my shoulders.

"Aaaah!"

"I said up!" he growled.

"Aspetti!" a voice from out of the crowd shouted. Wait! It must have startled Black Eyes because his grip on my arm slipped. I dropped to my knees on the pavement with another burst of pain and twisted around just in

time to see a tall figure break away from the crowd. I blinked quickly.

Seth?

Behind him, a hand reached out to pull him back. Pale skin. Short, dark hair. Seth's mom, Elena. Her eyes grew wide and her lips formed one word—'No!' Seth pulled away from her and she threw a frantic glance behind her. I followed its path, but from my low vantage point, I couldn't see much more than the top half of his head. Still, I knew it was Seth's dad, Victor, Elena was looking toward, pleading with her eyes. He didn't move.

Seth approached the police car slowly, holding his hands in plain sight. *"C'è uno sbaglio,"* he said. There has been a mistake.

The policeman turned with amazing speed and drew his pistol, leveling it at Seth's head. "The mistake," he said, "is yours."

CHAPTER
9

didn't know whether to laugh or cry. Seth was safe! Or at least he had been until he had the pistol pointed at him. I tried to push myself up, but I slipped and landed right back on my knees. Loose gravel on the cobblestones bit into my skin, but I didn't care. Seth was alive. That was all that mattered.

My chest literally felt like it was swelling as I stared at him, I was so happy. His skin had taken on a sepia tone since I'd seen him last, like he'd spent a lot of time in the sun. And his dark hair had gotten longer, the ends curling against his collar and wisping over his ears. His eyes were the same intense blue, though, and still had the power to make me feel warm all over.

I wanted to call out to him, but I knew better. He could be going under another alias, so it wouldn't be smart to use his name. I bit my tongue and watched helplessly as Black Eyes took an aggressive step toward him. He motioned with his gun for Seth to move forward.

"Hands on your head," he ordered.

Seth clasped his hands and rested them on the top of his head as he had been told. His blue eyes locked with mine as he walked toward the car. He was acting much calmer than I felt. When he got close enough, he reached down to help me up.

"Leave her, Romeo."

Seth ignored the guy and hooked a hand under my arm. I had just about gotten my feet under me when Black Eyes slammed his pistol against the back of Seth's skull. Seth crumpled and we both went down. I fell sideways against the car so that my arms pulled back at an odd angle and the metal of the handcuffs cut into my skin. Seth tried to push himself up, but swayed and collapsed again. I had to clamp my mouth shut to keep from screaming his name.

The man, who I can genuinely say I hated by then, prodded Seth with his foot. "You will listen when I speak to you," he said. *"Capisci?"*

A murmuring rose around us. Men in their shirt-sleeves grumbled and shuffled their feet. Mamas in aprons and head scarves watched with wide eyes and whispered behind their hands. But no one moved to stop what was happening. I no longer saw Elena or Victor. I wondered—I hoped—that they had gone to get help.

The policeman turned his black eyes on the crowd. *"Non c'è niente da vedere!"* he shouted. There is nothing to see here! He ordered them back to their homes. Seth he left lying on the cobblestones. He stepped over him like he was a sack of trash and grabbed me by both arms to drag me to my feet. "Get in the car," he ordered.

I considered resisting but I was afraid that if I made him angrier, he would take it out on Seth. I climbed awkwardly into the backseat while Black Eyes made Seth kneel on the road and place his hands on his head once more. Then he took each hand in turn and twisted it behind Seth's back, snapping on another pair of handcuffs.

"In," he said, pointing to the car. Seth struggled to his feet and then climbed into the back with me.

I wanted to throw my arms around him, but even if my hands hadn't been bound and I could actually reach for him, I knew I wouldn't do it. I pretended not to even recognize him as Seth settled onto the seat. Black Eyes hmmphed and slammed the door shut.

As the man walked around the car to the driver's seat, I looked to Seth and hissed, "What is going on?"

"I could ask you the same thing," he whispered. "What are you doing here?"

"I came to warn—"

Seth cut me off with a shake of his head as the front door opened. The policeman slid into his seat and started the engine. Then he turned to glance at the backseat and smiled. It was the most sickening smile I'd ever seen in my life.

Seth and I couldn't speak as we rode along. Even though there was a Plexiglas partition between the front and backseats, a little circle of small holes had been drilled through it, so it was not a soundproof barrier. I didn't even dare to look at Seth too closely because I could see the policeman's eyes in his rearview mirror as he drove, and he was watching us. I did slide my foot across the floor so that it was touching Seth's, and Seth pressed his leg against mine, but that was as much communication as we dared.

While Seth sat stoically beside me, my heart was doing ninety and my hands were slick with sweat. I needed to take a cue from his example and not let Black Eyes know that I was terrified. He seemed like the kind of man who would feed on my fears like a shark with blood in the water.

I stared out the window, trying to keep my mind occupied, but it didn't do much good. The passing landscape barely registered. I did notice obliquely a long stand of spear-shaped cypress trees at the edge of a green field, and the thought occurred to me that we were no longer in the city, but that's about as far as the thought process went. I was too busy worrying about how Seth's parents would know where we had gone. Wondering if Ryan had managed to rouse Agency support. Watching for any signs of imminent help.

In the front seat, Black Eyes began to hum. I didn't even recognize what the song was, but I immediately hated the sound. My stomach twisted as I considered who he could be. My guess was that he worked for The Mole.

I stole a glance at Seth and he met my eye for just the briefest of moments before he quickly looked away again. For that instant, a connection passed between us, powerful and real. He was afraid as well; I could feel it. But I could also feel that he was even more determined we would get out of this thing together. I shifted on the seat, moving closer to him, and felt tentatively behind me. My fingers found his and we hooked them together, drawing strength from each other.

It wasn't until I noticed that we were entering some kind of industrial area that I realized I hadn't been paying much attention to our location. I had been too focused on what was inside the car to spare much thought for what was outside. By the time I snapped to and remembered what my mom had taught me, too much distance had passed for me to get my bearings.

I twisted around in my seat to check out the back window. All I could see were the red-tiled roofs in the distance and what looked like a lake far over to one side of the road. The plants and trees in the open spaces looked wild and untamed.

"Where are we?" I whispered to Seth.

He shrugged and shook his head. Not good. He didn't know, either.

The policeman eased the car up to a closed gate. He inched forward until it slowly opened. Either the gate was on some kind of motion sensor—which wouldn't provide the greatest security—or he had a remote in the car, or maybe someone inside opened the gate. Only there didn't appear to be anyone inside. The place looked completely deserted as we drove along the short drive to the empty parking lot.

"The weekend," Seth whispered. "They must be closed."

I had no idea who "they" might be, but I had a feeling, judging from the weeds pushing up through the cracks in the parking lot and the broken windows in the building before us that the weekend had little to do with the desertion.

"What is this place?" I whispered. The building was maybe as long as two or three football fields with high, multipaned windows and a couple of smokestacks poking up from the rear. The bricks were black with soot and ivy snaked unchecked up the sides of the building. The tall letters on the side of the whitewashed walls proclaimed the business name to be GIORDANO.

He circled the car around one side toward a loading area with a long concrete dock with four distinct bays. Parked on the blacktop surrounding the dock were several cars and a couple of black SUVs. So the place wasn't deserted after all. In fact, as our car inched forward into one of the empty bays, a trio of men with guns materialized from behind double swinging doors and watched us with interest. I looked to Seth and could tell by the way he stiffened in his seat that he had seen them, too.

Black Eyes killed the engine and stepped out of the car, slamming the door behind him. He climbed up onto the dock and carried on a long conversation with the men with guns. I couldn't hear a word they were saying, but with all the effusive gesturing of hands and dark glances into the car where Seth and I waited, I could only guess that they were talking about us.

Finally, one of the men disappeared back through the swinging doors. When he returned, a cold seed of fear sank deep into my gut. He had not come back alone; trailing close behind was none other than the Marlboro Man. He shook our fake policeman's hand and together they approached the car. I sat frozen in my seat, unable to do anything but watch in terror as they drew nearer.

"That man," I whispered to Seth, but that was all I could say before the door opened. I hadn't realized how stuffy it had become in the backseat until a cool rush of air filled the space. I took a deep breath and gave Seth's fingers one last squeeze before he was pulled from the car.

I scooted toward the open door to follow him out when Black Eyes stopped me. "Not so quick, eh, *signorina*?"

All I could do was watch helplessly as he led Seth away. A cold sweat washed over me. I wanted to run after him, or at the very least demand to know where they were taking him, but I knew I shouldn't say a word.

When he had disappeared through the swinging doors, Marlboro bent down to peer at me through the open door. He smiled, showing teeth that had been stained a sickening brownish yellow.

"*Allora, signorina,*" he said. "You will come with me."

He reached inside the car and grabbed my arm, dragging me from the seat. Once again, I was struck by the bitter, burnt-tar-and-farm-refuse smell about him. I turned my head away from him so that I could breathe as he pushed me toward the crumbling concrete stairs leading up to the dock.

"Where are we going?" I demanded. He just grunted and propelled me up the stairs and across the loading dock to the double swinging doors.

I tried again. "Where's my friend?"

"Silenzio!" he barked, and pushed me through the doors.

Inside was some kind of interior loading area. Several wooden pallets lay scattered about, some still bearing bales of mildewing cotton. Stacked against the wall were dusty bolts of an indigo fabric. Denim, I realized with a jolt.

The room tilted and my head buzzed as if a million insects had been set loose in my brain. Denim. Caraday said it had been manufactured in Varese—that the textile mill had been closed for years. My eyes widened in terror as I looked around at the dilapidated fixtures in the room. If I had any doubts before, I now knew who had orchestrated my false arrest.

My stomach heaved as I realized that I was likely standing in the very mill that produced the denim used to bind and gag Lévêque before he was thrown into the river.

"This way." Marlboro yanked on my arm, indicating a long hallway crowded with wide, square rolling carts, all empty. A pungent odor hung in the air. Nothing terrible, just very strong. I wasn't sure what it was, but something about it smelled familiar. Like the scent that comes from ironing a cotton shirt. But mixed with the hot cotton smell and Marlboro's bitter stench was something much heavier. I guessed it might be the indigo dye they used on the denim, but I had no idea if I was right.

From the hallway, I could see a cavernous room, like an elephant graveyard full of old looms, some of them with cones of thread still attached.

He led me down a narrow corridor, the fluorescent lights overhead flickering a pale, sickly light. At the end of the corridor, he stopped in front of a black metal door and pulled a set of keys from his pocket. He unlocked the door and swung it wide.

"In," he said.

I peered inside the dark room. The heavy smell was even stronger in there. "What is this place?" I asked.

"You will have answers soon enough," he said, and pushed me through the door.

I stumbled inside and he slammed the door shut behind me. Except for a narrow sliver of light that bled in from the corridor, the room was entirely dark. I have a thing about the dark. Have had ever since Seth and I got stuck in a cave on the island and we had to literally feel our way out. Plus, there had been bats. I shuddered at the memory. I don't like not knowing where I am or what could be sharing the space with me. Logically, I knew there were probably no bats in the room, but there could be other vermin. Vermin that at any moment could jump on me and gnaw at my fingers . . .

I closed my eyes and made myself take several deep breaths, trying to let the tension out each time I exhaled. It didn't really work, as far as the releasing tension thing went, but it did help me to think a little more rationally. It wasn't going to do me any good to stand around in the dark freaking out. I slid one foot forward, and then the other, feeling my way along the floor until I found the wall. With my hands still behind my back, the only way I could feel for a light switch was to run my shoulder along the wall, so that's what I did. I started by feeling around the door first, and when that didn't yield any results, I searched farther out.

I'd made it halfway around the room with no success when suddenly the lights flicked on and the door opened behind me. I blinked against the sudden brightness and spun around. Marlboro had returned and he was not alone.

Next to him, with thick arms folded across an even thicker chest, stood a stocky woman wearing a tight, black business suit. "*Cosa sta facendo?*" she demanded. What you are doing?

I met her stare and squared my shoulders. "Looking for the light switch."

"It is in the hall. When we want you to have light, we will let you know." Her words were clipped, disdainful. I wondered what Marlboro had told her. "You will come here." She indicated a spot on the floor directly in front of her.

I crossed the room hesitantly. It's not like I had much choice. What was I going to do? Run away? To where? The loading dock with the gunmen?

"I must search for weapons," she informed me.

It took a full second to register what she meant. She was going to search *me* for weapons. That's why Marlboro brought a woman. I suppose I should have been grateful for that gesture of propriety, but I backed away. "Oh. No. I don't have any—"

"Stand still," she ordered.

I held my breath as she patted her hands along my arms and legs, and then along my sides.

"What is this?" she asked as her stubby fingers found the envelope tucked into the waistband of my shorts.

"Travel money," I said honestly.

She grabbed the envelope and turned it over in her hands, her face showing new interest. Her mouth twisted into a self-satisfied smile. *"Grazie,"* she said, and stuffed it inside her blouse. To Marlboro Man she proclaimed, "No weapons," and she marched through the door.

He waited until she had gone and then gave me an exaggerated bow. "You will come with me."

"Where are we going?" I asked.

"Enough." He grabbed my arm, his stench like a cloud that engulfed me. I wondered what it was in the tobacco the guy smoked that smelled so bad.

He led me back down the hallway into a huge room. I guessed it was the main section of the mill. The ceiling was probably three times as high as in the other room, crisscrossed with metal walkways above the work area. A row of windows, offices, I presumed, looked out over the workspace like skyboxes at an arena. I imagined bosses, stern as prison guards, watching from those windows, or strolling the walkways, making sure that the employees wove their quota of fabric.

From somewhere in those offices, strangely, I could hear strains of classical music. It seemed out of place in the shambles of the broken-down mill.

We rounded the corner of one of the huge loom machines to see Seth standing beside Black Eyes, presumably waiting for us. Seth looked up at me and gave me an encouraging smile, even though he had to know as well as I did that our situation wasn't good. It was all I could do to keep from running to him. That I wouldn't have been able to throw my arms around him didn't matter. I would have figured something out. As it was, though, I kept my distance, giving him a polite nod. There would be time for talking—and hugging—later. At least I hoped.

Seth and I were led up a set of rickety metal stairs to the walkways above. The angle of the stairs was steep and the stairway narrow—only one person wide—so we ascended in single file. As we climbed higher, I was able to get a bird's-eye view of the room below. Amid the machines, I could see several men and an occasional woman or two standing around, talking, watching us, working with some kind of wire—though I'm not sure what they would be doing since the mill was obviously defunct.

At the top of the stairs, Black Eyes motioned for us to stop. "You will stay here," he said, and left us with Marlboro Man as he ambled across the walkway and tapped on one of the office doors. He cracked open the door, spoke to someone inside for a moment, and then strolled back to where we stood.

"We will wait," he announced.

Marlboro reached into his pocket and pulled out a crumpled box of cigarettes and began to shake one loose.

"*Idiota!*" Black Eyes spat, knocking the package from his hands. He gestured with his eyes to the area below. Marlboro clenched his jaw and bent to retrieve his scattered smokes. Some of them rolled through the little spaces between the metal flooring and tumbled to the machines below and he cursed under his breath.

"Now," Black Eyes said to Seth and me, "you will come this way."

He led us across the walkway to one of the office doors

and rapped sharply. Without waiting for an answer, he opened the door and ushered us inside.

To my surprise, a gentleman sat in the corner of the room, playing a cello. I felt like I had stumbled into a dream. The man didn't look up, but continued playing his piece, eyes closed, swaying with the swing of his bow. The fingers of his other hand danced over the frets, pausing here and there, wavering to create vibrato. It was a beautiful performance. So why did it make me feel so uneasy? I glanced at Seth to see if he shared my apprehension and what I saw sent a slice of fear through my chest.

Seth's face had gone completely white. Even his lips had drained of color. He stared, wide-eyed, at the man with the cello, like he knew him. Like he was terrified of him.

Finally, the music ended, the last melancholy note hanging in the air before fading away. Only then did the man look up and smile. I was wrong about Black Eyes having the creepiest smile I'd ever seen. This guy upped the creepiness factor about a thousand percent. "Hello, Aphra," he oozed. His accent held a distinct Eastern European flavor. "So nice to finally meet you."

"I . . . I'm afraid I don't . . ." I looked to Seth again.

"Oh, yes. How rude. Mikhael, you haven't introduced me to your little friend."

At first I thought he was talking to Black Eyes, calling

him Mikhael, but then I remembered—Mikhael had been Seth's given name before his family had been forced into hiding. He told me once that he had been Seth so long that he preferred his new name to the old one. But if this man knew the old one . . . Suddenly, I felt like I needed to puke.

The cellist tsked. "I'm sorry, my dear. It appears Mikhael has forgotten his manners. I am Dominik Lucien Brezeanu, but you may have heard me called by my simpler name: The Mole."

CHAPTER
10

The Mole smiled his wicked smile and watched me like he was hoping for a reaction. I tried not to give him one, though I'm sure he could see the fear written on my face. I just stared at him, thinking that this distinguished-looking gentleman with his close-cropped silver hair and pale blue eyes was not at all what I had imagined when I pictured what The Mole might look like. I had imagined him as some kind of mob boss figure, wearing gold chains and smoking oversize cigars. But I guess evil is more effective if it comes wrapped in an attractive cover.

"It is a pleasant surprise to find you here," he said. "After this morning, I had quite given up meeting you. When my ... associates dropped in to pay a visit to young Mikhael's family, they were rather dismayed to find that they had already left the premises. Warned off by the Agency, were you?"

He directed his question to Seth, but Seth stared straight ahead as if no one had spoken. That made The Mole chuckle. "He's a stubborn one," he said to me, "but we'll soon break him of that."

The thought of how The Mole or his minions might try to break Seth made my knees wobble. I could have crumpled to the floor right then, only I was pretty sure that would have been just what The Mole wanted. I took a cue from Seth and focused my eyes on a crack in the plaster behind The Mole's head.

The Mole chuckled. "So much like your mother," he said. "Pity, that."

I couldn't help it. My gaze snapped right back to where he was sitting.

"I didn't realize you had accepted my invitation," he continued, methodically loosening the strings on his cello before laying it in its case. "I'm afraid I already released the horseman."

The room spun. The horseman . . . the fourth horseman . . . death. "What are you saying?" I asked.

"The message was quite clear," he said. "Either she would deliver you children to me, or she would die."

My stomach heaved. The words of the macabre message danced mockingly in my head. *Deliver the children lest he should ride.* I assumed—I think we all assumed— the note was a threat against the Mulos. It never occurred to me that if he didn't get his way, the monster would go after my mom.

"But, I'm *here*," I said weakly.

"Ah, yes." He closed the cello case and fastened the latches. "But not by the specified hour. And if my sources are correct, had it been up to your mother, you would not be here at all."

I stared at him. How could he possibly know that?

Maybe he didn't. Maybe he just knew that any mother with half a brain wouldn't say, "Oh, you want me to give up my kid? Sure. Here you go." ·

"She will learn," the Mole continued. "You will all learn—you myopic capitalists with your unmitigated arrogance. You will be brought to your knees soon enough."

"What does that have to do with my mom?"

"It has to do with your mother," he drawled, "because she works for the most corrupt government in the world. She has pledged her allegiance to an administration of money-grubbing plutocrats who have commodified the entire culture. She supports a monopoly of global wealth and power. She forgets what your government has done to our country. How their sanctions starved our children, how—"

"Give me a break," I muttered. "She got in your way, that's all."

Seth gave me a warning nudge. "Aphra . . ." he said under his breath.

"Ah, yes. You see? He is learning. He knows that it was *his* family who set us on the path that has led us here today. His parents who betrayed their fellow comrades in favor of baseball, hot dogs, apple pie, and an SUV. But they sowed the seeds of their own destruction, boy. My years in federal prison were the best education America had to offer."

The Mole plucked a scarlet cashmere scarf from the

side of his stool and draped it around his neck. "It's true, I would not have chosen my own incarceration, but those years proved to be most valuable. I learned to navigate the underground, to connect with the power of international organized crime. Prison could not subdue me; it only extended my reach. Now I have comrades all over the world. Signore Labruzzo here is part of that extended family."

Black Eyes—Labruzzo—inclined his head.

"I have your parents to thank for the wealth of connections, Mikhael. I discovered an entire world of criminals in federal prison, all looking for a little . . . direction." He studied his impeccably manicured nails and added in a bored tone, "Despite whatever personal benefit I may have gained, however, your parents betrayed me, and traitors must be punished."

Seth's jaw tightened, but he didn't speak.

The Mole, unmoved, looked to me instead. "And your mother must pay for her involvement in their corruption. Had the American government not resorted to deceitful tactics to obtain their treasonous accusations, we would not find ourselves in this situation today."

I clamped my own jaw tight and breathed hard through my nose. I was not going to let him goad me into talking back, even though I'd like to tell him a thing or two. But it wouldn't do any good. You can't reason with insanity.

"You must understand," he continued, "I abhor

violence, but there are times when a big stick is more effective than a soft word. Your parents killed twenty years of progress toward bringing down American dominance. They destroyed the cell I so painstakingly pulled together and nurtured over the years. So I find it a fitting addition to my statement that I destroy their creations." He spread his hands as if to encompass Seth and me.

"What statement could you possibly make?" Seth spat.

The Mole cocked his head, his mouth twisting as if amused. "My colleagues have been scattered. Many have been captured. But the work will go forth. My statement"—he paused for effect—"is to show that I will not be hobbled."

I didn't want to ask. I truly didn't want to hear the answer, but I had to know. "What have you done with my mom?"

"I have done nothing with her." His lips split in an oily smile. "Yet."

He was lucky that my hands were still stuck behind my back or I would have clawed his eyes out. I gritted my teeth. "Where is she?"

"Your mother is on her way to rescue her daughter."

"But she doesn't know where I am."

He arched a brow over one pale eye. "Why, certainly she does. The Agency is not exclusive in the use of bait."

My mouth went dry. "I—I don't understand."

'It's quite simple. Since you would not go to her in Milan, she is coming to you."

Icy fear licked the back of my neck until my hairs stood on end. I knew I was playing his game, but I had to ask. "How did you know I was supposed to go to Milan?"

His cold smile made my stomach turn. "I have my sources. Close, reliable sources." He winked and I thought I'd lose it right there.

What did he mean, "close sources"? Close to him or close to my mom? Who even knew? Ryan would never have given me up. And then my heart sank. Caraday. I remembered the way she whispered her instructions to me, how she said my mom was sleeping when I left. . . . That should have raised a huge red flag, had I stopped long enough to think about it. There's no way Mom would have gone to sleep unless she knew that the Mulos were safe. So either she already had a plan in play or Caraday had been lying to me. Or both.

"And my mom and dad?" Seth asked, though I'm sure he would rather not have heard the answer.

"Yes," The Mole said in his saccharine voice. "They have received an invitation as well."

He crossed his long legs and brushed imaginary lint from his trousers, signaling the end of his interest in our conversation. "Labruzzo, we must finalize the preparations. Kindly show our guests to their new accommodations."

Labruzzo bowed as if he were a manservant.

"Oh, and Labruzzo, one more thing. Please explain what will happen when the Mulos and Signora Connolly arrive for their children, would you?"

Labruzzo's lips lifted. He fixed me with his black eyes. "Boom," he said.

My legs shook as we crossed back over the metal walkway. I had to breathe through my nose, afraid that if I opened my mouth, I'd scream. The workers down below, the wires, suddenly it made horrible sense to me; they were rigging the textile mill with explosives.

I could barely climb down the stairs, but Labruzzo had no patience for my being slow and growled at me to hurry up. He marched us through the machine room and down a wide corridor lined with the same square bins I had seen earlier near the loading dock.

In front of a battered wooden door, he stopped, jangling the keys on a large brass ring until he found the one to undo the lock.

The door swung open to reveal a room that was only about ten feet square. Even more carts crowded the room, these overflowing with what looked to be cast-off fabric and scraps, all heaped in the corners and spilling out onto the floor. Bits of plastic and paper, old pins and thread spools littered the floor. The tall windows on the far side of the room were caked with grime and only let in a weak, yellowish light. In the small space, the strange smell was even stronger than in the open space of the factory.

"In," Labruzzo ordered.

I drew back. If he was trying to kill us with chemical fumes, he might not be far off.

Labruzzo grabbed my shoulder and gave me a vicious shove. I stumbled into the room, slipped on a piece of fabric and fell to the floor. Pain shot through my elbow and up my arm.

"Aphra!" Seth rushed to where I lay amid the trash and dropped to his knees, but there wasn't much he could do to help me.

The door clicked shut behind us, followed by a metallic clunk. Probably Labruzzo setting the lock again. At least Seth and I were together. And, for the first time since I first saw him in Varese, we were alone. It should have been our "moment." We should have been able to hold each other and comfort each other and tell each other that everything was going to be all right, even though it wasn't. By keeping us cuffed, The Mole had even taken that away from us.

Frustration and anger swelled inside with edges so sharp it brought tears to my eyes.

"Hey," Seth whispered. "What's wrong?"

I rolled onto my side so that I could at least look up at him. He leaned over me, his eyes—his beautiful blue eyes—so filled with tenderness and concern that I cried even more.

"Are you hurt?"

I could only shake my head.

"Then what's the matter?"

"I want to hug you and I can't," I choked out.

"Hold on a sec." He let himself topple over so that he was lying on the ground facing me and then wriggled like a worm so that we were face-to-face. His voice went husky. "I want to hug you, too," he said. That made me cry again, only happier this time.

"Hey, shhh . . ." he said, and rubbed his cheek against mine. His warm skin felt sandpapery and soft at the same time. I closed my eyes and nuzzled against him like a cat, breathing in the smell of him—an earthy blend of lime and soap.

"I've missed you so much," I whispered.

"You have no idea." He pulled back so he could see my face. "I've been going crazy. No one would tell me where you were."

"Me, neither."

"Where *were* you?"

"Lyon and then Paris."

"Only a few hours away. No wonder they wouldn't tell me. I would have found you."

"I would have found you."

"You did find me."

I smiled. "Oh, yeah."

We lay there looking at each other for several heart-beats, and then Seth leaned close and brushed his lips against mine. A wave of champagne bubbles burst open in my stomach, my head, my heart. I stretched my neck to reach him again, and he kissed me, deeper, longer. For those brief minutes, I forgot my pain and my fear. All I knew was that Seth was there with me. I nestled my cheek in the hollow between his shoulder and his neck.

And then I opened my eyes.

I had found Seth—and because of that, he was lying on the floor of an abandoned factory, manacled and marked for death. I swallowed hard against the ache in my throat. If what The Mole had said was true, my mom had set an alternate plan in play to get the Mulos to safety. If it hadn't been for me, they might have gotten away.

"Why did you come forward?" I moaned.

Seth pulled back and looked at me incredulously. "What?"

"When Labruzzo arrested me," I said. "He was making a show of it, trying to flush you out." Just like Caraday said we were going to do with the Mole. The irony only made it hurt worse. "Why didn't you stay hidden?"

Seth shifted so that he was angled toward me. "Aphra, look at me."

I raised my face to him again. His brows dipped low. "I would never let anything happen to you," he said. "I stepped out of the crowd because it was not possible for me to stand by and watch you be hurt."

"But . . . you could have gotten away. You could have been free."

He shook his head. "No, Aphra," he said softly, "I will never be free of you."

His cobalt eyes held mine and for that moment, everything else melted away until it was just Seth and me and that was all I needed. It didn't matter what awaited us or how we were going to get out of it. For that little time I could believe that everything was going to be all right.

I was wrong.

CHAPTER
11

could have lain there with Seth for hours, but our aching shoulders and the urgency of the situation wouldn't allow it. We needed to get out of the textile mill and warn our parents. With some difficulty, we pushed to our feet and stood together, trying to figure out a plan, trying to understand what had happened with each other to lead us to that spot.

"What happened this morning?" I asked him. "Before I got there."

Seth glanced back at the door, and then leaned close to tell me. "We were eating breakfast when a telegram was delivered. It was kind of a shock, since no one was supposed to know where we were."

"What did it say?"

"It was the message we dreaded getting for years, 'Send the books.'"

"I don't understand what that means."

"It's code. We had to learn the code before we went into hiding. If we get a message that says to 'pack the books,' we're supposed to make preparations to leave town. Pack a few things, maybe withdraw some money from the bank, but sit tight and watch and be on high alert. But if the message says to 'send the books,' that means to get out immediately."

"Oh." So the Agency *had* come to warn the Mulos. I should have trusted that they would, but I had to be sure. "Where did you go?"

"Nata—your mom had rented an apartment one building over. That was our safe place. She rented it with her own money so that no one would know about it. She figured that if we ran after someone discovered where we were hiding, they would never think to look so close."

That sounded like my mom. Be prepared. Trust no one. "If they didn't know about the apartment, where did the Agency think you were going to go when you got the 'books' message?"

He shrugged. "I hadn't really thought about that. All I know is that when we got the message, we had to clear out and go to the safe place and wait for instructions."

"So . . . once you got there, you were supposed to stay in the safe apartment, right? What made you come outside?"

Seth lifted one shoulder. "We could see the street from the window. That was something else your mom insisted on. So . . ." He let his gaze drop. "The police car caught my attention. I mean, he'd left his lights flashing so I figured something was up. I watched and when I saw him bringing you out of the building . . ." He looked up at me, face sincere and open. "I snapped. I ran out of the apartment and my mom ran after me. She tried to make me stop. And my dad followed her." His shoulders sagged. "They've probably been going crazy, trying to figure out where the police car would have taken us. I wonder how The Mole gave them the message where to find us?"

"He probably didn't have to. My mom would have gone to them immediately. They're probably all together." Which meant Caraday was probably with them and they didn't know she was in league with The Mole. A fresh surge of panic gripped me and I pulled my wrists against the handcuffs. "We've got to get these things off."

"Wait. Can you pick the locks?"

"Me?" I laughed. Well, not really a full-out laugh, but one of those "yeah, right" guffaws. "I've never even *seen* a set of handcuffs up close before now."

"But you have picked locks."

"Not these kind of locks." Back at the resort, I'd learned the basics of lock picking from our super, but we're talking about doors and cupboards. Handcuffs? No way.

"The concept is pretty much the same, though, right?" Seth persisted.

I chewed on my lip. I didn't share Seth's confidence, but it's not like we had a whole lot of other options. I might as well give it a try. There was only one problem. "What am I going to use as a pick?"

Seth scanned the room. "There's got to be something we can use in here. Let's look through the bins."

Without the use of our hands, even that simple task proved to be difficult. We had to turn around backward to dump the bins and then sift through the fabric scraps with our feet. It wasn't a very effective way to look for any object small enough to fit into a handcuff lock. Besides, if we happened to find something, how were we supposed to pick it up?

"This is going to take forever," I said.

"Let's split up." Seth pointed to the back corner of the room with his chin. "You take that corner and I'll take the other and we'll meet in the middle."

"I hope we're not still going at it long enough to reach the middle," I grumbled. Still, I slogged through the trash to my corner of the room and started looking.

We worked in silence for maybe five minutes when suddenly Seth jumped back from the bin he was about to overturn. "Holy crap!"

I spun around, expecting to see Labruzzo holding a gun on us or something. The look on Seth's face as he stared into the bin was equally as chilling.

"Aphra . . . you'd better come over here."

The tone of Seth's voice grabbed my insides and twisted them tight. "What is it? What's wrong?"

He shook his head, brows pinching together. "I think it's that guy . . . the agent from Seattle."

"What?" I rushed over to where Seth stood. There, half buried in rags, lay Ryan, his face slack and pale except for umber streaks of dried blood across his forehead and down one cheek. "No," I whispered. When I ditched him, Ryan had been on his way to meet my mom. If they found him . . . I stumbled backward, darkness creeping into the corners of my vision.

"Aphra? Are you all right?"

My lips parted but I couldn't find my voice.

"You think he's dead?" Seth's words sounded far away.

"I . . . I don't know." The way he lay crumpled in the bin, I couldn't tell if Ryan was breathing or not—and I couldn't check for a pulse with my hands stuck behind my back. I raised my eyes to meet Seth's. "Help me get him out of there."

Together, we carefully tipped the bin on its side. Ryan gasped in pain as he rolled out onto the floor. I let out a breath. At least he was alive. But I could now see the gash on the side of his head. That must have been where all the blood on his face had come from. Brighter, crimson blood matted his hair and soaked the collar of his shirt. He was still bleeding.

As if he could feel us staring at him, Ryan slowly raised his lids. His eyes rolled in their sockets until he finally managed to focus them on me. "Hey," he said. His voice barely registered above a whisper.

I bent over him. "How are you doing?"

He drew in a serrated breath. "Been . . . better."

Seeing him struggle to form the words made my heart lurch. "Shhh. Just lie still. We're going to get us out of here."

Ryan closed his eyes again, but his lips curved just enough to make me think he was trying to smile. He started to nod his head, but then winced and lay still again.

"That cut looks bad," Seth whispered.

"He'll be okay," I said automatically. I hoped it was true. It looked as though he'd been hit pretty hard on the head. He could have a concussion. Judging from his coloring and the amount of red soaked into his shirt and the rags around his head, he'd probably lost a lot of blood.

My wrists already ached where the edges of the metal cut into them, but I twisted and pulled my hands in frustration, trying to work the cuffs off. Trussed up as I was, there was nothing I could do to help Ryan. I couldn't wrap his wound. I couldn't make him more comfortable. I couldn't do anything. He drew in a deep breath and held it, wincing again when he let it out. I pulled against the cuffs even harder.

Seth bumped me with his shoulder. "Aphra, stop. Your skin's raw as it is."

When I looked up at him, I wanted to cry. In part because I felt so helpless, but also because of the concern and confusion I could read on his face.

"I've got to help him," I said. "This . . . this is all my fault."

Seth shook his head. "No. Don't start blaming yourself for—"

"But it's true. At first he was set to come with me to Varese but then I heard him talking on the phone. He was going to try and get me to go to Milan, so I ditched him. Then he had no choice but to come after me. If I hadn't been so stubborn—"

"I'm *glad* you were," Seth said. "If you hadn't been, I might never have seen you again."

I blinked back tears. "But I led them right to you! This is what The Mole wanted all along. I played right into his hands."

"Aphra. Stop it." Seth's voice became hard. "He used you, yeah. But what if you hadn't come? My family would have run again, but we would never have been free. He would never stop hunting us."

"I know." I thought of my frustration in Paris and I couldn't even imagine how sick of running Seth must be. "That's why I had to come."

His eyebrow cocked upward. "And here I thought you came to see me."

I allowed myself a smile at his attempt to make light of the situation. "That, too."

At my feet, Ryan moaned again. My smile faded. No matter what Seth said, I couldn't shake the feeling that Ryan wouldn't be lying on the floor if it wasn't for me.

When I stepped off the train to Milan, it was a pretty good guess he'd caught the next train to Varese to find me. If he hadn't come after me . . .

If he hadn't come after me, he would have shown up in Milan empty-handed. Knowing Ryan, he wasn't going to do that. Which meant he would have had to call someone to explain why we weren't coming. I sucked in a breath.

"What is it?" Seth asked.

"Someone knew where he'd be."

"What are you talking about?"

I dropped to my knees next to Ryan and nudged him. "Did you tell them you were coming back for me?"

He cracked an eye open again and tried to lift his head. "I . . . don't know what—"

"I heard the phone call. I know you were supposed to divert me to Milan."

His face went slack again. "Oh."

Seth's eyes flicked from me to Ryan and back again, confused, questioning. I turned away from him; I didn't want to explain about the shed.

"Did you tell them I got off the train?"

With some effort, Ryan nodded.

"So they knew that you were going to follow me."

He nodded again. "They said they would find us here."

I groaned.

"Wait. It could be a good thing," Seth said. "We need more numbers on our side. Maybe if—"

"No. Don't you get it?" My voice rose with my frustration, and Ryan shushed me. I stood so that Seth could hear my whisper. "It's just like The Mole said. He knew they were coming. Caraday must have told him. And she probably said where The Mole could find Ryan, too."

"No," Ryan said. "Not Caraday. She—"

"She gave us up!" My stomach twisted with anger. Seth was right; it wasn't my fault that we were there. The whole thing was one big setup. No matter what I did or didn't do, The Mole would have his endgame. He said that he'd released the horseman because Mom had not sent me to Varese as he had demanded, but that wasn't exactly the truth. I had come on my own. I had delivered myself. That should have changed the outcome, but it hadn't. It just changed the venue.

Behind my back, my hands curled into tight, angry fists. My mom was racing into a trap. Seth's mom and dad as well. Ryan lay bleeding on the floor with Seth and me manacled so we couldn't help him. I had reached my boiling point. The Mole had taken as much from me as I was going to allow.

From the moment my mom had become involved in helping the Mulos, The Mole had had a hold over our lives. I thought of all those years on the island, me believing that my mom hadn't come with us because she didn't want to when in reality, she was protecting us. She knew how ruthless The Mole could be. As long as he was after her, she'd had to stay away from us. The Mole had stolen four years from my family.

And what about Seth's? The Mulos had been on the run since Seth was in grade school. The Mole had chased them, taunted them, tried to kill them.

Like he had tried to kill my dad. My fingernails dug into the palms of my hands. Like he *had* killed Bianca. And Joe. And Lévêque, and I didn't even know how many others.

I thought of The Mole's smug smile as he hid like a coward in his little room above the working floor. He probably never did any of the dirty work himself. He just sat in the shadows, orchestrating, plucking strings. Well, I wasn't going to be played anymore.

"No more talk," I said. "Let's keep looking for something to get the cuffs off."

"Grab one of those . . . U pins," Ryan suggested.

The little silver pins were scattered across the floor. No doubt they'd been used to secure bolts of cloth. I couldn't believe that I hadn't thought of using one of them before. It's just that with those sharp points . . .

Ryan must have sensed my hesitation. "They're perfect," he assured me. "You just . . . break one in half. Use the . . . bent part as your pick."

Seth slid me a look. "Will that work?"

I couldn't help but laugh. "We've got a CIA operative telling us to use a pin and you're asking *me* if it will work?"

"I was just checking."

"Yeah," I conceded. "I think it will work."

We sat on the floor, each one of us feeling behind our backs blindly, fingers skittering over the trash in search of a pin. You'd think it would be easy, but it wasn't. Finally, Ryan had to push himself up onto one elbow to give us directions.

"A little more . . . left. Closer to you. Almost. Right there."

"Got it!" Seth whispered.

"Good." Ryan lay back down. "Break it in half at . . . the base so you have a . . . little hook on the end. Aphra, you move closer to him so he can reach your cuffs."

It wasn't easy, but I scooted backward so that my shoulders were touching Seth's. He reached out and found my fingers with his.

"Feel for . . . the round part of . . . the keyhole," Ryan said.

Behind me, I could feel Seth's head shake. "Aphra should do it—she's picked locks before."

Ryan raised his brows at me, lips pressing together like he was trying not to smile.

"Nothing illegal," I said.

He let the smile break free then, but it quickly turned to a wince. He sucked in a deep breath and let it out slowly. He didn't look good. We had to get him some help. Quickly.

I stretched my hand out and felt for Seth's. "Hand me

the pick. Carefully. I'll try." I stretched my fingers out to take the pick, but our behind-the-back coordination was not great. It dropped with a little *klink!* onto the floor. Seth tensed. I could literally feel his frustration building.

"It's okay," I assured him. "Just give me the other piece."

Slowly and painstakingly, we managed to transfer the piece of U pin from his hand to mine.

"Okay, I've got it." I said. "Now what?"

"Feel for the . . . keyhole," Ryan said. "It's round with . . . a little line coming from it."

I fingered the warm metal of Seth's cuff until I found the hole. "Yes, I've got it."

"Insert the hooked end into the hole . . . about one o'clock."

I fumbled with the pick to fit it into the circle part of the hole and felt around the mechanism. Like Seth had guessed, the feel was similar to other locks I had picked back at the resort, just much, much smaller. I pushed and twisted and pulled the pick and nothing happened. Again and again and again I tried until my hands grew slick with sweat. The sharp end of the pin-pick poked my fingers and the metal cuffs chafed against my wrists. Meanwhile, Ryan was losing more blood. Getting weaker.

"It's no use," I cried. "I can't do it."

Seth curled his fingers up around mine. "It's okay. Just relax. You can do this."

Warmth spread upward from my fingers and swelled in my chest. I know it sounds sappy, but if Seth had so much faith in me, I wasn't going to let him down. I closed my eyes and felt for the latch with the pick again. Once, twice, three times. Finally, I felt it move. "I . . . I think I got it."

But nothing happened.

"Why won't it open?"

Ryan blew out a long breath. "It's probably double-locked."

"What?" Panic squeezed my throat like a fist. "What does that mean?"

"Calm down." Ryan's voice dropped and he shot a glance at the door. "It's nothing to worry about. Double-locked cuffs . . . have a kind of a bolt that keeps the ratchet from moving. You've managed . . . to release one. The second will be easier."

Easy. Sure. Now if I could only make my heart stop racing around my chest and keep the sweat from soaking through my shirt.

"Aphra, look at me." Ryan's eyes met mine, steady, sure. "All you have to . . . do is find the narrow straight part that . . . runs upward from the circle."

I nodded, clamping my jaw tight, and jiggled the pin until it slid into the secondary slot. Ryan was right about it being easier; I got it after only four tries. With a click and a metallic scrape, the handcuff swung open on its hinge.

"Yes! Thank you!" Seth whispered. He twisted around and drew me into a backward hug, the handcuff swinging from his left wrist.

New pain shot through my shoulders from the pressure and I shied away. "Watch the arms!"

He drew back. "I'm sorry. I wasn't thinking."

"It's okay. I'm just a little . . ."

My voice trailed off as I caught sight of Ryan. He had dropped back into the rags, face sweaty and pale. He gave me a weak smile.

"Seth." I pointed to Ryan with my chin. "His head."

Seth touched the handcuffs on my wrists. "Will you be all right for a few more minutes?"

I forced a smile of my own and tried to ignore the throbbing ache in my shoulders. "I'm fine. Take care of Ryan."

Handcuff swaying, Seth quickly sorted through lengths of cloth on the floor until he found a piece long enough and clean enough to wrap around Ryan's head to try and stop the bleeding. He had just finished tying the knot when he stiffened, head cocked like a Labrador.

"What is it?" I whispered.

"Do you hear that?"

Without waiting for an answer, Seth jumped up and tiptoed to the door. He pressed his ear against the worn paint and listened.

"It sounds like they're leaving."

I struggled to my feet and ran over to the door. Sure enough, I could hear muffled voices, fading footsteps, car engines revving up, doors closing. They were scuttling out of the factory like rats abandoning the ship. Which could mean only one thing.

We were running out of time.

CHAPTER

12

Seth turned to me, dark brows drawn low. "We've got to get out of here."

"You think?"

"Give me the pin so I can get those cuffs off you."

The pin. It had been in my hand when I rushed to meet Seth at the door. My stomach tumbled right down to my knees. "I dropped it."

Panic and irritation clouded his face, but he drew a deep breath, like he was sucking in calm. "It's okay. It's okay." I wasn't sure if he was assuring me, or himself. "We'll make another one." He scanned the floor for more U pins.

"Seth," I said, my voice small. "We have to stop them."

He halted his search and stared at me as understanding dawned. If The Mole's people were leaving, that meant that the endgame was near. It meant that my mom and his parents were getting closer. And when they came looking for us . . .

Seth must have been thinking the same thing. "But how would they find this place? We're out in the middle of nowhere."

I shook my head at the irony. The Mole was using us

as bait, which was exactly what my mom hadn't allowed me to be. "I'm sure he left plenty of bread crumbs for them to follow. Besides"—I gave Ryan a sharp look— "I'm guessing we're on GPS."

Ryan raised his eyes to meet mine. He held my gaze for a long time before he nodded miserably.

"Wait." Seth shook his head in confusion. "What?"

"I should have figured it out earlier," I said. "The Agency does like its techno toys." Back in Seattle, one of my mom's old partners had boasted about putting tracking devices in everything.

Seth threw a sharp look at Ryan. "He's got a tracker on him?"

"Either that, or I do," I said.

Ryan closed his eyes. "How ... did you know?"

I took a deep breath before speaking. Until that moment I hadn't been sure, but all the pieces were fitting into place. "You wouldn't believe the rules I had to follow with my mom," I said. "No phones, no e-mails, no friends. Keep to yourself, watch your back, don't draw attention to yourself. We should have been invisible. But somehow you knew exactly where to find us."

"Lévêque ... could have told us you ... were meeting in the park," Ryan countered.

"True. But you didn't find me in the park. You were waiting in the train station. Lévêque couldn't have told you I was going to go there. He was ... dead." My voice caught on that last word.

"My job is to protect you. I had . . . to know where you were. . . ."

I took a step closer and stared him down. "Where is it? My wristwatch? No, it would be too easy for me to leave behind. My earrings maybe?" And then my breath caught. "My shoes."

Ryan hesitated and then he nodded.

I closed my eyes, shaking my head as I thought of how easily Lévêque had gotten us to take the shoes. How excited I had been to have them. "You embedded something in the shoes so you could follow me."

"Your mom, too," he said sheepishly. "We were afraid she would take you and go into hiding again and we wouldn't know where you were to protect you."

"You're such an idiot."

Seth stared at my Pumas, his fists tightening again. "They're going to follow your *shoes* to find us?"

"Yeah," I replied. "Ironic, isn't it? Caraday probably tipped off The Mole about the GPS and from that moment on, we were walking targets."

Ryan just shook his head. Not like he was denying it, I don't think, but like he couldn't believe it had happened. He looked so bewildered that I almost felt sorry for him. Not Seth, though. He rounded on Ryan, injuries or no.

"What were you thinking? Did it never occur to you that The Mole could use your own technology to track her as well?"

"He shouldn't have known. Shouldn't have . . ." Ryan leaned his head back against the rags and closed his eyes.

"What I don't get," Seth said, "is why they left Anderson here alive." He glanced at me. "I can see if he needed to follow you to find out where my family was, but what did they need him for? After he passed along the bugged shoes, why didn't they take him out right there?"

My mouth dropped open. "Nice, Seth. Real nice."

"No, he has a point," Ryan said weakly. "This . . ." He let his gaze wander around the room. "The entire thing is a game. Remember what . . . Caraday told you. The Mole is a psychopath. We all . . . crossed him one way or another. He's gathering us . . . together. To punish us."

A metallic taste spread through my mouth. I felt like I was going to throw up. It was a game. A game! My mom, Seth's parents . . . racing to save us, but running straight into a trap. So he could have his amusement. So he could have his revenge. He was so sick, watching us like rats in a cage. Arranging every little detail. Every little detail . . .

I groaned. "She must still be wearing her shoes."

"She what?"

"Her shoes. Her shoes! The GPS things! They're tracking my mom. That's how they know where she is. And if they're clearing out, it means she's close. And when she gets here . . ."

Seth's eyes met mine. "Boom."

● ● ●

Seth was right about his not having the touch to pick locks. Even with Ryan patiently instructing him, he couldn't get that first lock. "I'm sorry," he kept saying. "I'm sorry."

"It's okay," I told him. "Really. I know how hard it is."

But that didn't make him feel any better. Especially when Ryan reached out to me weakly and said, "Come here. Let me try."

I couldn't see Seth's face because he was behind me, but I heard the little disappointed huff as he dropped his hand. I caught Ryan's eye and gave him a slight shake of my head. "No, Seth. You almost had it," I said. "Give it one more shot."

Ryan pressed his lips together, nodding as if he understood. I wasn't sure I did. Understand what I was doing, I mean. Since we didn't have a lot of time to mess around with, letting Ryan undo the handcuffs would have been the smart thing to do. But something told me that Seth needed to be the one to do it. I had to go with my gut on that one.

Finally, I heard a tiny *click*. He'd gotten the first lock. "The second one is easier," I assured him. "Much—"

"Shhh!" Ryan hissed. "Seth, down! Put your hands behind your back."

I could feel Seth's hesitation, but only for a heartbeat. He dropped to the floor just as the door swung open. Labruzzo's tall frame filled the doorway.

"Ah. You found him," he said.

I followed his line of sight to where Ryan lay, eyes closed, on the pile of scraps. When neither Seth nor I responded, Labruzzo grunted and took a couple more steps into the room. "You, *signorina*," he said, pointing to me. "You come with me."

A rush of icy fear swept through my veins. "Where are we going?"

"You'll see soon enough."

"I'll go," Seth said. I twisted around to see him rising to his knees.

"It's the girl I need," Labruzzo said. His oily voice slid over my skin and made me want to retch.

"She's not going," Seth said.

Labruzzo just laughed. "I don't remember asking your permission, Romeo." He grabbed my arm and yanked me to my feet. I bit my lip to keep from crying out from the pain.

"She's not well," Seth said, now standing.

I took his cue and feigned a cough. All that accomplished is that Labruzzo's grip tightened, his fingers digging into my skin like talons. "I don't really care." He pulled me closer to him.

I thought I might puke all over his shiny black policeman's shoes. One thing I knew; there was no way I was going to let him take me out of that room even if he dragged me. Which gave me an idea. I went limp. Because he had such a tight grip on my arm, my dead weight pulled him off balance.

That was all Seth needed. He jumped forward and swung his arm with the handcuffs still attached and caught Labruzzo right in the face. Unfortunately, handcuffs, even at a high rate of velocity, have only so much force. The impact didn't take Labruzzo down as much as I wished it had. It did, however, catch him off guard and he dropped me like dirty laundry as his hand slapped to the welt on his face. He snarled in pain and anger.

I had fallen to my knees so that I was facing away from him, but I could feel him close behind me. And I knew that it was only a matter of nanoseconds before he recovered from the shock of the handcuff whip. And then he would go for his gun. I didn't even think—because if I did, I might have hesitated, considering what I was aiming for. Like a slingshot, I swung forward and then threw all my weight into a back-of-the-head head butt to his groin.

The air whooshed out of him like a punctured tire. He doubled over and I rolled to the side so that he wouldn't fall on me. But he didn't fall at all. Stumble, yes. Curse a blue streak, yes, but hit the ground, no. All we'd succeeded in doing was to make him very angry. As I had feared, his hand immediately went for the gun at his waist.

Dead, cold fear swept over me. All I could think at that instant was that Labruzzo was going to kill Seth. I didn't care what came after. A low growl escaped my lips, so feral that it surprised even me. Labruzzo's head turned just as I kicked out at him. He danced away, leveling his gun at me.

The distraction was enough for Seth to swing his handcuff nunchuks again, this time clocking Labruzzo across the top of his head. Labruzzo roared and swung the gun toward Seth. I coiled my legs back again. I knew I had only one more shot at him and if I missed, Labruzzo would probably kill us both. I kicked out with every ounce of anger, pain, and fear I had bottled up inside and my foot connected with his knee with a sickening *thunk*.

Labruzzo fell to the ground, bellowing like a wounded bull. The gun tumbled from his fingertips and before he could reach for it, Seth snatched it from the ground.

"Down!" Seth yelled, brandishing the pistol with chilling disregard for someone who had not even been able to handle a gun just a few short months ago. But he didn't have to worry; Labruzzo's eyes rolled back and he passed out.

"Good work," Ryan said.

Seth's head shot up, as if he had forgotten Ryan was there.

"Get Aphra's cuffs off. We have to . . . get out of here."

Seth looked at me like he was in shock. Now that the action was over, the gun trembled in his hand. His fearlessness had been a bluff.

"The hard part's over," I assured him. "The second lock is easy."

His face crumpled. "I lost the pick," he said.

I could have laughed if he wasn't so serious about it. "That isn't the first one we've lost. Just make another one."

"But hurry," Ryan put in.

I shot Ryan a look to let him know he wasn't helping. He shrugged as if to say "what?" but I didn't miss the shadow of a smile on his lips.

Seth made his pick and to his credit, he was able to open up the cuff on the first try. I sighed with relief as I brought my arms forward, rolling my shoulders to relieve the tension. An angry red band circled my wrist where the cuff had been. I rubbed at the soreness with my other hand.

"Undo Mulo's other one," Ryan said.

I glanced down to where Labruzzo lay moaning on the floor. "Maybe we should just get out of here."

"We don't want . . . to leave him loose."

He had a point. I eyed Labruzzo again, wondering if I should just check him for keys. That would be much easier than fiddling around with an improvised tool. But he wasn't completely out and I wasn't about to get close to him by myself until his hands were good and secured. "Seth, hand me that pick."

It was much easier picking the lock when I could actually see what I was doing, but still it took several tries before I was able to pop that elusive first lock. By the time Seth was completely free of the handcuffs, Labruzzo was starting to stir.

Seth grabbed one of his arms. "Help me get him over by the pipes."

I hesitated, but he gave me another one of his earnest looks. "I won't let him touch you."

Together we dragged Labruzzo across the floor. Seth snapped a cuff around one hairy wrist and then fed the chain behind the pipe before twisting Labruzzo's other hand back and cuffing that one, too.

"Get his . . . keys," Ryan said. "And cell phone . . . if he's got one."

I reached forward to check Labruzzo's front pocket, but Seth stopped me. "I'll do it," he said.

By the time he had been relieved of his personal property, Labruzzo was starting to come to. He opened his eyes slowly, painfully. When the understanding of his predicament registered on his face, he rattled his hand-cuffs against the pipe. *"Porca miseria!"* he cursed.

"Yeah, that's right," I assured him. "You are a miserable pig."

Seth pulled my arm. "Come on, let's go. We'll have to help your friend over there."

I didn't miss Seth's sour expression at the mention of Ryan, even though it lasted for only a fraction of a second. "Wait." I turned back to Labruzzo. "Where are they?"

He didn't say anything, but his black eyes fixed me with a stare so cold I felt like I needed a jacket.

I shook off a shiver and bent so that I was eye level with him. "This place is wired, right? So where are the explosives?"

He raised his chin and made a big show of clamping his mouth shut.

"Fine." I stood. "Your decision. Hope you can live with it when we're gone and it's just you and the explosives."

He stared straight ahead and pretended not to hear me. Idiot. I turned to Seth. "Let's get out of here."

CHAPTER
13

Seth and I each took one of Ryan's arms and slung them around our shoulders and practically carried him from the room. He barely had the strength to stand, let alone walk. I noticed with a sick twist in my stomach that the rough bandage around his head was completely soaked through. No wonder he was so weak; he was still losing a lot of blood.

"What now?" Seth asked.

"We have Labruzzo's keys," I said. "I think we should get out of here. But should we call someone first? Tell them what's going on?"

"With . . . Labruzzo's phone? No." Ryan said it with such incredulity that I felt really stupid. I had already considered the possibility that his phone was tapped or traceable or whatever you call it, but it's not like I was talking about carrying on a personal conversation. Just a simple "hi, don't come to the textile mill because it's going to blow up" sounded good. But I had to defer to Ryan's judgment. He was the operative, not me.

We had made it as far as the loading dock before Seth drew to a halt. "Wait. What about your shoes?"

"My what?"

"Your shoes. You know, the tracking things. You leave here with them on, The Mole can see wherever we're going."

I pulled them off like they were on fire, but then I realized that if I left a locating device at the factory, my mom would follow the signal to find me, which is exactly what The Mole wanted her to do. Seth was right, though; I couldn't take them with us, either. I stared down at my shoes. All that time I'd been running around in them and I had never even guessed that I was being tracked by the CIA, let alone by The Mole and his minions. "Can we just . . . turn it off?" I said to Ryan. "The GPS thing, I mean."

"There is . . . no off."

"Then we'll smash it or something. Which shoe's it in?"

"Both."

"Where are they? Can I pull them out and—"

Ryan winced. "They're . . . built into the . . . sole."

Of course. Leave it to the CIA to make things complicated. I took a deep breath and let it out my nose before I spoke. "Fine." I chucked one shoe across the loading dock. "We'll split them up at least. We can dump the other one somewhere down the road. Maybe the confusion will be enough to keep Mom from bringing the rescue squad here until we can warn them. Let's go."

I helped Seth half guide, half carry Ryan down the

concrete steps to Labruzzo's car. Ryan leaned heavily against me as Seth jangled the keys, trying and rejecting them one by one in the car door. "It's not here."

I peered over his shoulder. "What's not?"

"The key to his car."

"But . . . he used his keys to drive us here."

"Maybe he has another set."

Ryan was getting heavier. I don't know if he was starting to sag more or if I was just getting tired, but whatever the case, he needed to get help quickly. We needed Labruzzo's car.

"Can you hot-wire it?" I asked Seth.

"What makes you think I can hot-wire cars?"

"I don't know. Because you lived in Detroit?" I said, repeating the explanation he had given me in Seattle when I questioned how he knew how to break into a car.

"Sorry, I flunked Auto Heist 101."

I almost didn't want to ask, but I did, anyway. "So what do we do now?"

Seth sighed and looked back toward the loading dock. "I'll go see if he has another set of keys."

"What? No. Not alone." I turned to Ryan to ask if he'd be all right if I ran back inside with Seth, but Ryan's face had gone slack. His eyes were closed. "Oh, crap. Seth, help me!"

Seth climbed up onto the loading dock and wrestled one of the bales of cotton free from a pallet and heaved it so that it landed just feet from the car. It burst open on impact, sending tangles of stale cotton in all directions. He jumped down after it and piled enough of it together that we could lay Ryan down in relative comfort.

He took my hand but after only a few steps he stopped and looked deeply into my eyes. "I need you to know," he said, "no matter what happens, I'm glad you found me again."

I squeezed his hand. "So am I," I whispered.

He nodded, like that made everything all right. "Let's do this."

We crept back up the stairs to the dock and through the swinging doors. I clung to Seth's hand, dreading the necessity of looking into Labruzzo's black eyes again, worrying with every step that the place was going to go up like a Roman candle. Since I had abandoned my shoes, I had to be extra careful to watch for stray pins, for which I was almost grateful. It was a good distraction from the growing fear rising like a tidal wave above me.

When we reached the refuse room door, Seth glanced at me once more. His reassuring smile warmed me completely through. He pushed the door open and in an instant the warmth evaporated.

The wave came crashing down. An empty pair of cuffs lay on the floor near the pipes. Labruzzo was gone.

The seriousness of our situation came to me in stages. My first reaction was completely visceral. My mouth went dry and my heart raced. A cold sweat prickled from the back of my skull down the length of my spine. Labruzzo was loose and he was angry. I thought of Ryan lying alone and defenseless outside. Next came the terrible realization that my GPS Pumas were on the loading dock, beckoning my mom and Seth's parents and anyone else foolish enough to come help us. And the building was a ticking time bomb.

"What do we do now?" I whispered.

"We get out of here," Seth whispered back. We retraced our steps. Desperation clawed its way up my back. Where would we get out *to*? The factory was out in the proverbial boonies. We had no transportation. And, since I hadn't been paying attention as we made the drive from the city, I wasn't even sure where we *were*.

But all those worries came to an end as we turned the corner toward the loading dock. Because they were eclipsed with a much greater concern.

"I'm very disappointed in you," The Mole said, aiming a much nastier-looking pistol at us than the smaller version Labruzzo had carried.

Labruzzo himself stood just behind The Mole, sneering at us like a playground snitch. One of his eyes had completely swollen shut, which made him look even more menacing, if that was possible.

"Perhaps you didn't understand your role in my soiree this afternoon," The Mole drawled. "Your presence is required to make it a truly memorable occasion."

I just stared at him, mind racing. If he was able to appear so quickly after we had escaped the refuse room, he must have been close. Close enough to see us on the loading dock—unless Labruzzo had a way to summon him without the cell phone. And if he was standing there trying to impress us with his genteel speaking manner, then he must not be too concerned about the explosives going off. Which meant that either we had plenty of time before the factory was set to blow or perhaps that the explosion would be set off remotely.

The second thing that struck me was that The Mole was the one physically standing there in front of us, holding the gun. In the past, he was simply the one pulling the strings, leaving the dirty work to his minions. But now they appeared to be gone and he was the one with his finger on the trigger. Aside from Labruzzo, The Mole was confronting us alone. Marlboro Man wasn't even there to back him up. Maybe Ryan and Caraday were right; The Mole was psychotic. Everything else he might pawn off to his minions, but killing us—*that* he wanted to do himself.

Finally, it hit me that The Mole hadn't said anything about Ryan. Cold fear washed over me as I thought how we had left Ryan passed out and helpless. I slid a quick peek at Labruzzo's car and though I could see tufts of cotton stirring in the breeze, there was no sign of Ryan.

I opened my mouth to ask about him, but then swallowed my questions with my fear. I would wait. Watch.

If the Mole had done something to Ryan, he wouldn't be able to help boasting about it. If not, the last thing I wanted to do was alert The Mole to the fact that Ryan was no longer where we had left him.

Just then, The Mole's pocket beeped. He drew out a BlackBerry and glanced down at it. "Ah. Our guests are arriving."

I couldn't help myself. "Guests?" My mom. Seth's parents. I felt sick inside.

The Mole ignored me. "Signore Labruzzo, if you would."

Labruzzo stepped forward, my Pumas dangling from his fingers. He had tied the shoelaces together and he draped them over my shoulders like a derby winner's roses.

"Come with me," he said.

Seth's grip on my hand tightened. "She's not going anywhere."

The Mole's lips split into a sickening smile. "And what do you suppose you are going to do about it?"

Wrong question to ask. In one fluid movement, Seth yanked my hand, pulling me behind him, and swung a kick to catch The Mole in the gut. "Run!" he yelled.

I hesitated. Because in that instant, two things happened—The Mole dropped both his gun and his BlackBerry and reached for Seth with his bare hands, growling like a rabid wolf, and Labruzzo jumped forward to help his boss. What Labruzzo did not do was draw a gun, which told me that he was unarmed. The gun we had taken from him must have been his only weapon.

I whipped the shoes from around my neck and swung them with everything I had at Labruzzo's head. One shoe caught Labruzzo just above the ear. He turned and snarled at me, but I had already followed through with the first swing and brought the shoes around a second time. Before he could lunge at me, the shoe hit him smack in the face. This time he was quick enough to reach up and grab the shoes before I had a chance to swing them around again, but while his attention was on yanking the shoes from my hands, I kicked my knee up and caught him in the soft center of his solar plexus. He folded like a snuffed cigarette, bending forward just enough for me to smash both hands down on the back of his head.

Labruzzo dropped to one knee, but he wasn't done fighting. He grabbed my leg and tackled me as he went down. I fell hard on my behind, and Labruzzo grunted his satisfaction. Unlucky for him, I didn't have time to waste with him. Next to us, The Mole had grabbed Seth by the throat. Seth was swinging and landing what looked like some pretty good blows, but The Mole's grip only grew stronger. I didn't even think about it; I coiled my free leg up and let loose, kicking Labruzzo square in the temple. He dropped like a rock, body draping over my leg. I kicked him again to get loose and then scrambled on all fours away from him.

By then, The Mole had Seth in a headlock. I lunged for the gun, but The Mole must have seen me going for it because he kicked the gun and it flew off the loading dock in a black metallic arc. I could hear it clatter on the driveway below. I would have gone after it, but Seth's face was beginning to turn purple. He clawed at The Mole's arm, horrible gagging sounds escaping his lips.

"Stop where you are or I break his neck!" The Mole screamed at me.

I froze.

"Now stand up. Slowly."

I did as I was told.

"Very good," The Mole said. "Please place your hands on your head."

Seth locked eyes with me. "Run," he mouthed. "Now."

I didn't know what to do. Would The Mole hurt Seth if I bolted? Would he *not* hurt Seth if I stayed where I was and did everything he told me to? The answer to the second question was no. The Mole was all about hurting Seth and me as much as possible. Which meant that I didn't have much incentive to stand there taking orders. But I didn't want to leave Seth at The Mole's mercy, either. I had to give The Mole a good reason to abandon Seth and come after me.

I stepped backward and my foot hit the BlackBerry. The contact was like a bolt of lightning shooting through me. I knew exactly what I needed to do.

CHAPTER
14

In that instant, everything began falling into place in my mind, like pieces to a puzzle. Labruzzo kept us locked up in that room so that the GPS in my shoes would bring my mom to the factory, but he sat down at the end of the hall so that he could make a quick getaway when my mom and her entourage arrived. The Mole hung around, watching, waiting for the perfect moment to detonate his explosives. He would want to watch, that was certain, so he would be using a remote electronic device. Like a BlackBerry.

I stooped down and swept up the phone, stuffing it into my shorts pocket, and then spun and ran back through the doors into the factory.

It took only a second to see that I was right. I didn't stop to look back, but I could hear The Mole toss Seth aside and come after me.

I rushed into the huge room with all the looms. The Mole's heavy footsteps rang out behind me. I dodged between the machines, in and out of the shadows, deeper and deeper into the mill.

"Stop," he yelled.

Ha. He wasn't even gaining on me. One of the distinct

disadvantages of having other people take care of your business, I suppose. He should have been more active.

And I should have been more careful. I wasn't watching the ground ahead of me. In the next instant, white-hot pain slashed through my foot. I fell hard to my knees and twisted around to see a shard of metal about the size of the BlackBerry I had stolen sticking out of the bottom of my foot. My stomach lurched and I had to swallow hard to keep from throwing up. Running through an abandoned factory without shoes . . . not smart.

I didn't even want to look at the thing, let alone touch it, but I knew the metal would have to come out. Breathing deeply, I gripped the shard with shaking fingers and pulled.

"Aaagh!" The cry ripped straight up from the center of my gut before I could stop it. I pressed my lips together, but it was too late. I'd given away my location. I could hear The Mole's footsteps slow and change direction.

Dropping the metal shard, I dragged myself behind one of the looms. The Mole must have seen that I had gone down, because he quit running. I could hear him, kicking through the debris on the factory floor, making his way to my hiding spot.

I pulled my knees close to my chest and pressed my back flat against the side of the loom, but it didn't matter how invisible I tried to make myself; a smear of blood trailed behind me, marking my position. All I could do was listen to the heavy scrape of his shoes drawing nearer. I held my breath, hoping he would pass me by.

He didn't.

The Mole stepped around the corner of the loom, grinning down at me like a demonic jack-o'-lantern. "Hello, my dear."

I scrambled to the side, hoping to crawl under the loom to get away, but he stopped me, stomping hard on my leg. I screamed in pain.

"Give it to me," he said.

"Give what to you?"

"You know exactly what." He held out his hand. When I didn't move to give his BlackBerry to him, he ground his heel into my leg. I cried out again.

"This is not a game, little girl," he said. "Where is it?" His face contorted in rage.

"I don't have it," I said.

The heel pressed down, down.

"I threw it away while I was running!"

Grind.

I howled.

"Give. Me. The. Phone."

But there was no way I was going to do that.

He stomped down and I heard my own bone snap. Pain rolled like thunder up my leg, followed quickly by a wave of nausea.

"I don't have it!" I screamed. Of course, he and I both knew it was only a matter of him bending down to take it from the pocket of my shorts. But after what I'd done to Labruzzo out on the dock, maybe he didn't want to get that close.

He raised his foot again.

"I wouldn't do that if I were you."

"Back away from the girl, Brezeanu."

I twisted around to see both Seth and Ryan, side by side, guns leveled at The Mole. He froze where he stood, but only for a moment.

"You will die for this," he growled at me, and then dived behind one of the looms.

Seth looked torn. His muscles coiled taut and his eyes darted back and forth, watching for movement. I understood exactly what he was feeling. It had to end. As long as The Mole was alive, we would never be safe. But Seth wasn't a killer. He might be able to hunt The Mole down. He might even be able to pull the trigger, but then he'd be as haunted the rest of his life as he would be if The Mole were still on his trail.

Ryan must have sensed it, too. "Get her outside," he barked. Like he was giving an order. Like Seth didn't have a choice.

Seth hesitated for only a moment more. Then he stuffed the gun into his waistband and stooped down to scoop me up in his arms.

Over his shoulder, I locked eyes with Ryan. "Thank you," I mouthed.

He nodded brusquely—a motion that caused

considerable pain, judging from the way his jaw clenched in reaction to it—and then turned his attention back to finding The Mole.

We had taken only a few steps when The Mole's words rang out like the voice of God, nowhere and everywhere all at once. "You think it's over?"

Seth spun, searching the shadows. I buried my face in his shoulder to keep from crying out from the movement.

Ryan raised his gun with both hands, though I could tell he had no clear target.

"You amateurs! You nothings!" From the disdain in his voice, I could practically see the sneer on The Mole's face. "You think I wouldn't have planned a fail-safe? You think you're home free because you stole a *phone*?" He laughed. Not the wicked, confident laugh of a master criminal, but the shrill cackle of a madman.

I clung to Seth. "He's insane," I whispered.

Seth didn't say a word, but held me tighter, cupping the back of my head as if he could protect me.

Ryan backed to where we were standing. "This place is wired like Times Square at Christmas. Get her out," he whispered to Seth. "Now!"

Seth turned toward the docks and I watched over his shoulder as Ryan crept down the rows of looms, gun raised and ready. And then a shadow moved, just out of my range of vision. I gasped and gripped Seth's shoulders.

"What is it?"

A dark figure leaped from behind a loom and rushed toward the staircase. Ryan spun and fired, but the shot went wide. The Mole clambered up the metal stairs, Ryan close behind. My eyes snapped up to the window of the room where we had first seen the Mole that morning. His sanctuary. His lair. The fail-safe! That's where it would be.

"Ryan!" I screamed. "The room!"

At the sound of my voice, The Mole turned his head, slowing him down just enough for Ryan to dive for his ankles. The Mole crashed to the walkway, flailing his feet. Ryan grabbed one of his legs and held on to it like a bucking bronco. He shot an angry look to where we still stood in the room below.

"Mulo! Get her out of here!"

"No!" I cried. I tried to wriggle out of Seth's arms. "Help him!"

"Mulo!" Ryan yelled.

Seth's arms tightened around me and he ran down the corridor to the loading dock exit. We pushed through the swinging doors and he drew up short. Bright headlights lit the dock, punctuated by red and blue flashes from half a dozen police cars. The muzzles of several guns immediately pointed toward us, clicked and ready, and a confusion of voices ordered us in both Italian and

English to freeze before Mrs. Mulo's voice rose above them all. "Seth!"

The guns lowered. From out of the glaring lights, Victor and Elena Mulo rushed forward, arms outstretched. My mom wasn't far behind.

And then a shot ripped through the air and chaos broke out on the docks again. Seth dropped to the ground, and I tumbled from his arms, fresh pain shooting up my leg.

"Secure the perimeter!" someone yelled.

"It came from inside!" another voice answered.

The burnt-tar smell filled my nose and for a moment I thought I must be imagining things until I lifted my head to see a pair of snakeskin boots. I screamed and pushed myself backward until I realized that Marlboro Man was lying facedown on the dock, his hands tied with plastic handcuffs behind his back. His face was turned away from me. But right next to him lay Labruzzo, trussed like a Thanksgiving turkey. He glared at me with his good eye and mouthed, "You're dead."

That's when I passed out.

I was only vaguely aware of what happened next. I heard a voice cry, "Get them down from there!" I could feel myself being carried and coddled. I recognized my mom's voice, but I didn't know what she was saying to me.

I caught only a few of the words that were flying around

me. "... still in there." "... a lot of blood." "... without alerting the local authorities." "... broken leg." "... in the van." I was aware of hands. Hands prodding, comforting, tying my leg to a splint. Dressing the wound on my foot. Reaching into the pocket of my shorts.

My eyes flew open. Caraday. I grabbed her hand. "No! Don't you touch it!"

Mom was at my side in an instant. "Aphra, what is it? Are you all right?"

I could only stare at Caraday, who stared back at me with wild green eyes. "She's working for him!" I cried. "Don't let her have it!"

Caraday shook her head and exchanged a worried glance with my mom. "I think she's delirious."

"No! I know—"

"Honey, relax," Mom pressed my head back down. She didn't believe me.

I struggled against her. "Where's Ryan? He can—"

Caraday spoke to someone behind me. Someone I couldn't see. "Can't you give her something?"

"No." I struggled against her grip. "No! Don't ... you understand? Caraday ..." I lost the rest of my statement in a haze of pain.

Caraday's voice was gentle, so gentle. "It's going to be all right, Aphra. It's over. You did it."

I pushed her away again. "Seth!" I yelled. "Seth!"

"She's going to hurt herself," I heard Caraday's voice say. Where did my mom go? Where was Seth?

Hands came at me. Held me down. I felt a sharp prick and then my arm was flooded with warmth, followed by a disconcerting numbness.

Someone reached into my pocket and took the BlackBerry and I was powerless to stop them. I think I cried, but I'm not sure.

"Go!" I tried to warn everyone, but my mouth could barely form the words. "We need to get out of—"

But the rest of the sentence was blown away in the force of an explosion so strong, it sucked the air straight from my lungs. I gripped someone's hand—I hoped it was my mom's—and prayed we would get out alive.

CHAPTER
15

The first thing I saw when I woke was my leg, wrapped in plaster, and suspended from a series of pulleys and cables above the bed. It hurt too much to turn my head, but I took in as much of my surroundings as I could with my eyes. Railing on the bed. Pink plastic pitcher and a cup with a bendy straw on the nightstand. Weak sunlight filtering through Pepto-Bismol–pink curtains, the rest of the room stark, white. A hospital. Mom slept in a chair in the corner, her mouth hanging open as if in silent protest.

The events leading up to the hospital came back to me in small pieces, not necessarily in order. The Mole playing his cello. The Mole crushing my leg. Ryan's head. Seth cradling me in his arms. Caraday reaching for the BlackBerry. Labruzzo looking up at me with his one good eye. *Boom.*

Mom woke with a start, as if she could hear my thoughts. She saw that I was awake and rushed to my side. Her hands had been wrapped in gauze, but she stroked my hair with the backs of her fingers. "How are you doing?"

I tried to speak, but my throat felt raw. The words came out in a hoarse whisper. "I'm sorry for leaving, Mom."

Her smile trembled. "You did what you felt you needed to do," she said. I noticed that she didn't say I was right to sneak away from her.

"Where's Seth?"

"He'll be in shortly. He didn't want to leave until he said—"

"Leave?"

She stroked my hair again. "The Mulos . . . were never here, you understand?"

It hurt too much to shake my head, so I just stared at her.

"There will be an inquiry. We don't want them to be part of that process."

"What happened?"

"Agent Caraday recovered a BlackBerry that we believe belonged to The Mole."

"Where is it?"

"It was destroyed in the explosion."

That part I remembered. That would be why Mom's hands were bandaged. Why my throat was so raw. "She tried to blow us up," I said.

"What are you talking about?"

"The Mole. She worked—"

"You're tired. We can talk about this la—"

"Where is she?" I demanded.

"She's in the ICU," Mom said finally. "She's had a rough time of it."

"Serves her right."

"Aphra!" The softness left Mom's voice. "Why would you say such a thing?"

"She was trying to kill us."

Mom's eyes flashed. "Agent Caraday was trying to *save* you. That device you were so carefully guarding was a bomb. You owe her your life."

"But she—"

"I know." Mom cut me off. "She sent you to Varese against my wishes. I was none too pleased with her about that. But the minute she found out Lévêque had been leaking information to The Mole, she told me everything. She called Ryan and tried to stop you and when she couldn't—"

"Wait. Lévêque?" My stomach flipped upside down. "*He* was working for The Mole?" The world I thought I knew was suddenly thrown into negative images—black gone white, and white, black. Nothing made sense anymore. I shook my head. "But . . . he's dead."

"An unfortunate result of his association."

"But . . . why? Why would they kill one of their own?"

Mom shook her head. "These kind of people, life holds no value to them. Lévêque must have outlived his usefulness."

I sank back into the pillows. Lévêque deserved what he got, didn't he? So why did it make me feel so sad?

"What about Ryan? Did he get out? Is he—"

"Don't worry. He sustained some burns and a nasty concussion, but he'll recover."

"And The Mole? Did you find him? Did he—"

She nodded gravely. "He's dead."

"So it's over," I breathed.

She stroked my hair back with the tips of her fingers. "Yes, Aphra. It's finally over."

"*Scusate, signora.*" A nurse in colorful scrubs stood in the doorway. "There is a phone call for you."

Mom stood. "I'll be back." She bent to kiss my forehead before she left the room, just like she used to do when I was a little girl. "Rest now," she said. A lump rose in my throat and I didn't trust myself to say anything, so I just listened as the *clack, clack, clack* of her heels against the hospital tiles faded away.

I must have slept because when I opened my eyes, the pink curtains had been pulled back and sunlight flooded the room. I moaned and slammed my eyes shut again.

"Hello."

I bolted wide awake. Ryan sat at the side of my bed in a wheelchair, watching me. I was suddenly overcome by a very strong urge to pull the blankets up to cover my hideously ugly hospital gown. Not that he looked much better, head and hands wrapped like a mummy's, the gauze splotched and yellow in spots. What skin I could see on his face was an angry red and greasy with ointment. His eyelashes were completely gone. At least he was dressed, though, wearing a loose, white shirt and pull-on slacks. "Going somewhere?" I asked.

He tried to grin, but winced when the skin around his mouth wouldn't let him. "I gotta get back to work. I'm still on the clock."

"No, seriously. Are you okay to be discharged? You're looking kinda green."

"Ah. That." With effort, he shrugged. "They aren't . . . authorized to give me certain pain medications in here. Don't know what secrets I might divulge."

"But you're . . ." I gestured to his bandaged state.

"I'll be fine. I'm being transferred to a military hospital where they will give me plenty of lovely drugs. In fact"—he gestured gingerly with his head— "Mario and Luigi out there are waiting to deliver me right now."

I glanced to the hallway where a couple of burly men in sharply pressed white uniforms stood like twin Roman statues glowering at us, caps tucked under their respective hairy arms. "You sure they're not hauling you into some prison somewhere?"

"Have you ever *seen* a military hospital?" He tried again to smile.

"So you're really okay? The last I saw you—" I closed my eyes. I didn't even want to think about it.

"I'm good," he said quickly, and then leaned forward in his wheelchair, the fake leather seat squeaking beneath his weight. "Listen, I just wanted to tell you that you did a great job."

"But I got it wrong."

He shrugged—as much as he could, anyway. "So did I. But the important thing is that we got it right in the end."

"I *didn't*, though. I would have—"

"There's no going back, Aphra, only forward. Don't worry about what might have been. What's important is what *is*. You helped to bring down a dangerous organization. You should be proud of that."

I pleated the sheet between my fingers, trying to think of the appropriate response since I thought he was completely wrong.

"I was serious in Seattle when I said you should consider following in your mom's footsteps. You'd make a good operative."

"Oh, no. I—"

"Just think about it. Let me know if you ever change your mind."

"I won't," I said.

Someone tapped on the door. I glanced up and went all warm inside. Seth stood there, hands dug deep into the pockets of his jeans.

Ryan nodded to him. "Mulo."

Seth nodded back. "Anderson." He took a couple of tentative steps into the room and looked past Ryan to where I lay. "I just . . . came to say good-bye," he said.

Ryan backed his wheelchair away from the side of my bed, gesturing for Seth to take his place. "Sure. I gotta take off, anyway." He reached out a bandaged hand, and Seth shook it carefully. "Good luck to you, Mulo."

Seth gave him one of those tough-guy raise-the-chin-to-acknowledge-the-statement things. "See you around."

With one last glance at me, Ryan rolled out of the room. Seth stood watching me for a moment and then approached the bed warily, almost shyly. "How's the leg?" he asked. "Your foot?"

But I didn't care about those things. "Where are you going?" I blurted.

He perched on the edge of the mattress and picked up my hand. His fingers were warm and rough against mine. "We're going home," he said. He pasted on a smile, but it couldn't mask the sadness in his eyes.

I almost didn't dare ask. Given their past experience, I could imagine—now that the Mulos were free to come and go as they pleased—that the last people they would want to know their whereabouts would be the Agency. Or the offspring of the Agency. But I had to know. "Where's home?"

He looked into my eyes for a long time and then touched his free hand to my chest. "For me, it will always be right here." Then he looked away, as if he was embarrassed by what he'd said. The light from the window lit him from behind, giving him an almost ethereal appearance—unearthly and beautiful . . . and impossible to hold on to. When he raised his blue eyes to mine, I wanted to cry.

"My parents miss their families," he said softly. "They haven't seen them for over twenty years. . . ."

"How long will you be there?" My voice sounded small, pathetic.

"I don't know how long they'll stay." He cleared his throat. "I plan to start college as soon as I can."

"Where?" I whispered.

He lifted one shoulder, watching me from under his dark lashes. "Depends on where I get in. I don't exactly have regular transcripts to offer."

I laughed to hold back the tears. "Yeah, I can see the admissions board now, reviewing your extracurricular activities . . ."

"They wouldn't be able to see them." He grinned. "The file would be sealed."

"Even better." I laughed at the thought. "You'd be a man of mystery."

"James Bond!"

"Ha! Maxwell Smart." My smile quickly faded and I closed my fingers around his. "I'll miss you."

He raised my hand to his lips. His breath was hot on my skin. "I'll miss you, too."

I couldn't hold it back anymore. A single hot tear escaped and rolled down my cheek.

"Hey. What's this?" Seth cupped my face in his hand and wiped it away with his thumb. "Your meds must be getting to you."

If I could have sat up, I might have held him close and

hidden the rest of my tears on his shoulder, but with my leg strung up in the air, the most I could accomplish was to reach out for him, sobbing like a baby.

He gathered me in his arms and curled around me like a leaf. "You know," he said in a husky voice, "guys hate it when girls cry."

"I'm sorry," I sniffled.

"No. That's not what I meant to—" He held me away from him. "I was just trying . . ." He growled in frustration. "Look, you're not getting rid of me this easily, all right? I'll be back. I just don't know when."

I could only nod and grab handfuls of his shirt to pull him close to me once more. I closed my eyes, wanting to capture that moment in my memory forever, to tuck it close like a photograph so that I could take it out and relive it again and again and again.

Mr. Mulo came to the door and cleared his throat. I held Seth tighter.

"I'm so glad to see you're doing well, Aphra," Elena Mulo's voice said.

I released my stranglehold on Seth and looked up at her. *Well?* I was dying inside. "Thank you," I murmured.

"It's time to go now, Seth," she said softly.

I reached up to touch his face one last time. He held my hand against his cheek and turned his head to kiss my palm.

"Don't worry; I'll see you sooner than you think." He

laid the kiss in my hand flat on my chest, over my heart. He didn't have to say the words.

"I'll be waiting," I whispered. And then he was gone.

Mom and I flew back to the island together. I wasn't sure how Dad would be, seeing her again. I think he felt just as hurt and abandoned as I did when Mom stayed with her job instead of coming with us when we moved to the resort. But when he understands what she went through to protect us, maybe he can forgive her. And maybe if he knows how much I just wanted our family to be together again, he can forgive me for lying to him, for disappearing. I've learned that if you love someone enough, you can figure a way to deal with almost any situation.

I talked to Caraday before we left Italy. If she figured out that I had thought she was a traitor, she never let on. She got a medal of commendation from the Agency for what she did in Varese. I hope that makes her feel better about the scars she will carry for the rest of her life.

Me, I'm working hard on my homeschool packets. If I complete enough of them, I might be able to start sending in college apps this summer. I don't know yet where Seth will be going, but I figure if my grades are good enough, I can be accepted anywhere.

I guess that's one good thing my mom taught me through this thing: *Be prepared for whatever may come.*